Spicy Trade

Other Books Published by Author

We Think Therefore We are

Father Turned Monster

Spicy Trade

Dr. Ahmed Sayeed

ZORBA BOOKS

ZORBA BOOKS

Published in India by Zorba Books, 2018

Website: www.zorbabooks.com
Email: info@zorbabooks.com

Copyright © Dr. Ahmed Sayeed

ISBN Print Book - 978-93-87456-73-0

Zorba Books Pvt. Ltd.(opc)
Gurgaon, INDIA

Printed at Repro Knowledgecast Limited, Thane

Dedicate my book to Hindu India
it gave me life and much more

CONTENTS

ACKNOWLEDGEMENT

In Hinduism *vidya* or education is vital if one want to attain the four aims of human life namely virtue, wealth, pleasure and liberation. An illiterate is considered equivalent to an animal because without knowledge there will not be able to rise above his or her physical self. An individual who is educated is believed to be able rise above his or her physical self. An individual who is educated is believed to be able to rise who is educated to be twice born. The first time born physically and the second time spiritually. Although the education is encouraged, knowledge is believed to be double edged sword. If an amoral or evil person gains knowledge, it can be destructive force. They might misuse the power and bring misery to themselves or others. It is believed that the basic difference between a God and demon is the way they used their knowledge. A god uses his knowledge for the welfare of the worlds and demon uses his for own selfish aims. Because of this is a part of this education, students are taught to follow the path of gods and to develop virtue under the careful direction of their teachers so that they can continue on the path of righteousness for the rest of their lives as well as contribute to the welfare of the Society. I acknowledge with great gratitude to my esteemed and revered teachers

The Hindu scriptures recognized two types of knowledge, the low knowledge and the higher knowledge. The lowest knowledge includes the knowledge gained through personal experience and self-realization. Of the two the higher knowledge is preferred because it liberates people from the cycle of births and deaths, however no one can live by knowledge alone. That was the Teachers of ancient period taught their students. For this type of education that Vedic teachers preached and I am proud of myself for having born in this glorious India, the land of non-violence and tolerance where in the highest knowledge is imparted. This treatise is dedicated to India my native Country who gave me so much culturally.

PROLOGUE

Nationalism may be a belief but it is an applied belief for those who have born in particular space that is geographically bounded with. They owe very much to that land called home land and that home land becomes his patent rights to live as a member of that society and that space becomes his/their mother land. It is therefore become one's creed or political ideology that involves an individual identifying with or becoming attached to one's nation. Nationalism involves national identity by contract of Patriotism which involves the conditioning and personal behavior that support State's decision acts. From political or sociological point of view there are two main perspectives on the origins and basis of nationalism. One is the primordial perspective that describes nationalism as reflection of the ancient and perceived evolutionary tendency of humans to organize into distinct grouping based on an affinity of birth. The other is modernist perspective that describes nationalism on a recent phenomenon that requires the structural conditions of modern society in order to exist.

An alternative perspective to both these lineages comes out of engaged theory, and argues that while the form of nationalism is modern, the content and subjective reach of nationalism depends upon "primordial" sentiments. There are various definitions for what constitute a nation, however, which leads to several different strands of nationalism. It can be a belief that citizenship in a state should be limited to one ethnic, cultural, religious or identify group or that multi-nationality in a single state should necessarily compromise the to express and exercise national identity even by minorities. The adoption of national identity in terms in terms of historical development has commonly been the result of response by influential groups unsatisfied with traditional identities due to inconsistency between their defined social order and the experience of that social order by its members resulting in a situation of anomie that nationalists seek to resolve. This anomie results in a society or societies reinterpreting identity retaining elements that are deemed acceptable and removing elements of deed unacceptable, in order to create a united community. This development may be the result of internal structural issues or the result of resentment by existing group or groups toward other communities' especially foreign powers that are or are deemed to be controlling them.

CHAPTER 1

WHY NATIONALISM IS IMPORTANT?

Nationalism is a political social, and economic system characterized by the promotion of their interests of a particular Nation, especially with the aim of gaining and maintaining sovereignty (self-governance) over the homeland. The political ideology of nationalism holds that a nation should govern themselves, free from outside interference and is linked to the concept of *self-determination* and maintaining a *national identity* based on shared social characters such as *culture* and *language*, religion and politics and a belief in common *ancestry*. Nationalism, therefore seeks to preserve a Nation's culture by a way of *pride* in national achievements and society linked to *patriotism* which in some cases includes the belief that the nation should control the country to country's Government and means of production.

Nationalism can be a belief that citizenship in a state should be limited to *ethnic* cultural religions or identity even by minorities. The adoption of national identifies in terms of historical development has commonly been the result of a response by influential groups unsatisfied with traditional identities due to inconsistency between their defined social order and the experience of that social order by its members, resulting in situation of *anomie* that nationalism seek to resolve. The anomie results in a society of Societies reinterpreting identity, retaining elements that are deemed acceptable and removing elements deemed unacceptable, to create a unified community. Nationalism means devotion for the nation. It is sentiment that binds the people together. National symbols and flags national anthem, national languages, national myth and other symbols of national achievement and identity are highly important in Nationalism.

Nationalism is a '*newer*' word in English. The term dates back from 1844, although the concept is older. Glenda Stuga notes that "Twentieth century a time of profound disillusion meant with Nationalism was also the great of Globalism".

But Nationalism has been a recurring facet of civilization since ancient times, through the modern National political and self-determination was formed in the 18th Century. Examples of Nationalist movements can be found throughout the History, from the Jewish revolts in 2nd century to the reemergence of Persian culture during Sassanid of Persia, to the emergence of Latin Culture in the Western Roman Empire, during 4th and 5th centuries as well as many others in modern times examples can be seen in the emergence of German Nationalism as a reaction against Napoleonic control of Germany as a confederation of the Rhine around 1805-14. Linda Colley in Briton, forging the Nation 1707-1837 explores how the role of nationalism emerged about 1700 and developed in Britain reaching full form in the 1830's. Typically historians of Nationalism in Europe begin with the French Revolution (1789) not only for its impact of French Nationalism but even more for its impact on Germans and Italians and on European intellectuals. Even America's Revolution is an early is an early form of Modern Nationalism.

This political convulsion of the late 18th Century associated with American and French revolutions massively augmented the widespread appeal of Patriotic Nationalism. The Prussian Scholar Johann Gottfried Herder (1744-1803) originated the term in 1772 in Treatise on the Origin of language stressing the role of common language. He attached and exceptional importance to the concept of **nationality** and **patriotism**—"He that lost his patriotic spirit has lost himself and the whole world about himself" whilst teaching that "in certain sense every **human perfection is national**. Geographical space matter, but the identity of those who occupy such space may increasingly bedevil generations. Lesson: those who write about geo-politics should not only look back ward to 19th or 20th century world of Nationalist people fighting each other for space, but more contradictory world of over lapping identity where elemental battles for space will nevertheless still matter.

When someone say He is an American, that means something very specific is it not? It connotes a specific land space, historical experience a set of cultural proclivities and value system, Right? Indeed it has been asserted friendly that all American Jews, Catholics, Hindus, Muslims are nevertheless voluntary protestants because it is the Protestant creed and work of ethics which they have all sincerely subordinated themselves in the course of immigration and naturalization. This is all true, of course. However it is also true that American charter is itself changing and becoming, perhaps more subtle. But these are negative views which include.

However, for some scholars and intellectuals like Gene Callahan writes "My own view of nationalism is far more negative than theirs. Indeed I believe that nationalism is second only to communism as the greatest evil of modern politics. It is a cause of Mass murder and repression" Somebody ask that "Do we need nationalism to promote good causes? For that negative Nationalist says "We should do what we can diminish its influence in playing with Nationalism is like playing with fire. It is why because it develops the negative social elements like communalism, regionalism, racial feeling. In reply Gene Callahan states that "Nationalism, but, in my view is ethno nationalism". Further he states that "as I understood the term ethno Nationalism asserts only that we who are living here as citizens, American or India and that the foremost end of a national Government to protect us and our rights." This idea doesn't imply any hostility toward people from other countries. It simply means that it is their government that are tasked with protecting us and promoting of our wellbeing. Nationalists are certainly not families and their citizens are not children but in some respects ***there are useful apologia between the two*** that I recognize that I am firstly responsible for caring from my own children doesn't not mean I am hostile to other people's children or that I am pedophobia."

Bret Trump, Lapin, who are right wing populists lead the revolt against "globalism". Armed with powerful identity narratives, they seek to define "*Who are we*" are nativists nationalist or even racist. But Mare Saxes state" Progressive on the other hand, seem hard pressed to offer powerful collective identity narrative for the society as a whole. However, I am of the view that "the luxury of blissful ignorance is no longer possible"

Mao se dung writes about nationalism "Can a communist who is internationalist, at the same be a patriot? We hold the he not only can be but *also must be*. The specific content of patriotism in determined by historical conditions. There is the "Patriotism" of the Japanese aggressor and there is our "patriotism". The communist of Japan and Germany are defeatist with regard to the wars being waged by their countries. To bring about the defeat of Japanese aggressors and of Hitler by every possible means is in the interests of Japanese and German people and the more complete the defeat the better…. for the wars launched by aggressors and Hitler are harming the people at home as well as the people of the world. Chinas case however is different, because she is the victim of aggression. Chinese Communist must therefore *combine patriotism with internationalism.* We are at once internationalists and patriots, and our slogan is "Fight to defend the mother land against the aggressor." For us defeatism is crime and to strive for victory in the war as of resistance is an incapable duty. For only by fighting in defense of motherland we can defeat the aggressor and achieve national's liberation will be possible for the proletariat and other working people to achieve their own emancipation. The victory of China and defeat of invading Imperialists will help people of other countries. Thus in wars of Nationalism liberation *Patriotism is applied Internationalism*".

On other occasion he asserts that "What kind of spirit is this that makes a foreigner selflessly adopt the cause of the Chinese people's liberation as his own? It is the spirit of internationalism, the spirit of communism, from which every Chinese communist must learn….We must unite with proletariat of Japan, Britain, US Germany, Italy and other capitalist counties, before it is possible to overthrow Imperialism to liberate our nation and people and to liberate the other nations and people of the World. This is our Internationalism, the Internationalism with which we oppose both narrow nationalism and narrow patriotism.

According to Rolee of Chinese communist party in the National War October 1938) Selected works VolII.P.91).

However, to my dismay I find Laureates like Albert Einstein who argues in *haste* that "Nationalism is an infantile decease. It is measles of Mankind"

For that one discussion between two persons of England is purported and presented herewith.

Question from **A**: How long have you been away from your country?"

Reply from **B**: Almost since 7 years.

A states that "Then you have probably forgotten all about it.

Quite contrarily he further said that *"Even if my country does seem to have forgotten me, I have always thought of it"!*

Dr. B R. Ambedkar, writer of Construction of India states that "I do not want that our loyalty as Indians should be in the slightest way affected by any competitive loyalty whether that loyalty arises out of our Religion, out of our Culture and out of our Language. I want all people to be *Indians first Indians last and nothing but* Indian.

CHAPTER 2

INDIA IN THE CONTEXT OF NATIONALISM

Dr.Subramanyan Swamy, MP. In his article states that "Every Nation must have an identity to be regarded distinct. Even in USA a relatively young nation created by an influx, by an activity of an American Harvard Professor Samuel Huntington has penned a book titled who are we? Every country has its salience and substance. Salience which is the important that the citizens attributes of national identity over the other many sub identities. Second identities which is what the citizen think they have common, and which distinguishes them for others of other countries. We in India today do not have to conjure up a contrived identity, because saliencies imbedded in the concept of *Chakravarthin*, which **Chalukyas** had spelt out with great clarity, while substance is that Hindus have always searched for and found unity in other in all our diversities there in, thanks for our spiritual and philosophical people, which we now called as *Hindutva*. "

The whole world has known our vast territory and millions of the in habitants for centuries and called as or Hindu and Hind or as the Chinese know us even today both as Nation and people as "*yindu*". The root word in these terms is 'Hindu' which is the word for Persians. Arabs and Europeans meant a people living beyond the Sindh River and for the Chinese living beyond Himalayas and bounded by the Indusagar (Indian Ocean).

The world know us in these millennium not as nomads but as a highly civilized people who produced exotic goods the world has never seen before and who were hospital to visitors from abroad. There is a list of contents which unfold what India is and the list will follow few paras later.

Mr. Jonah Blank, an American Journalist curious about this Hindutva, took journey in 1991-92 from Ayodhya to

Srilanka on the route taken by Lord Rama. He then wrote about a book Titled: Arrow of the Blue skinned God-Retracing the Ramayana. He writes that "India is a land may be ruled by aliens from time to time, but never her mind, never her soul… In the end it is always India that does the digesting (p.217). He concludes "But somehow a nebulous sense of "Indian-ness does exist and it bids together Guajarati's, Orissa-ns to Nagas who might seem to have nothing in common. Perhaps it is the elusive, undefinable link that has allowed the sub-continent's multitude of races to live in *rough resemblance* of harmony for 4000 years."

The Territory in which Hindus lived was known as Hindustan that is specific area of a collective of persons who are bounded together by this Hindu-ness. The salience thus was given a religious and spiritual significance by Thirthyatra (pilgrimage), Kumbha Mela, Pushkar, common festivals and in the celebrations of the events in mythology viz. Ramayana and Mahabharata. Hindu Rashtra thus defined is our nation that is modern Republic to day, whose roots are also in the long unbroken Hindu Civilizational History. Throughout this history we were a Hindu Republic and not a monarchy (a possible but weak exception being Asoka's reign).

In the ancient Republic concept, the king did not make policy proclaim the law and state policy and the king implemented it. Hindu hence is our nature while Hindustan is our territorial body, but Hindu Rashtra (States) is our Republican soul. Hindutwa embodies all these aspects. This is the only way that Hindustan can become modern Hindu Rashtra. The parameter of Hindu theology. Hinduism is not a theology founded on the revelation of any single prophet or constituted by single scripture that which all adherent have to blindly believe in. It is instead *an accumulated wisdom of sages through centuries* that has been four Vedas, Upanishad 18 puranas two Ithihasas etc. There in Hinduism no "Church" or "Masjid "to belong to and obey its dictum or to believe in Pope, nor is there the likes of a Koran, Hadith or Surah in Hinduism to look good the faithful in the name of submission to God, to commit as His direction for violence against unbelievers termed as Kaffirs and Dhimmis. Therefore that is no scope for Hindu to be a fundamentalist.

Let me bring to the notice to the realm of remembrance of our readers that is how our India or Indian-ness is being clapped with emotional tears on witnessing her immortal achievements by other peoples of other nations. India gave following significant Science and technology discoveries by ancient Indians to the world:

(a) *The Decimal system*: India gave the ingenious method of expressing all numbers by means of ten symbols-the decimal system. Due to the simplicity of decimal notation.

(b) *The idea of Zero*: Little needs to be written about the Mathematician Aryabhatta was the first person to create a symbol of Zero and it was through his efforts that mathematical operations like additions and subtraction started using the digit. The concept of Zero and its integration into the place-value system also enabled one to write numbers, no matter how large, by using only ten symbols.

(c) *Numerical Notations*: Indians, as early as 500BC has devised a system of different symbols for every number *one to nine*. This notation system was adopted by the Arabs who called *hind* numbers. Centuries later this notation system was adopted by the Western world who called the Arabic numerals as it reached through the Arab traders.

(d) *Fibonacci Numbers*: The Fibonacci numbers and their sequences appear in Indian mathematics as Matrameru, mentioned in Pingala in connection with Sanskrit tradition of prosody. Later on the methods for the formation these numbers were given by mathematics of Virahanka Gopal Hemachandra, much before the Italian mathematician Fibonacci introduced fascinating sequence to Western European Mathematics.

(e) *Binary Numbers*: It is the basic language in which a computer programs are written. Binary basically refers to set of two numbers 1 and 0 the combination of which called ***bits and bytes***. The binary number system was first described by the Vedic Scholar Pingala, in his book Chandra Hastra which is the earliest known Sanskrit treatise on prosody (the study of poetic meters and verse).

(f) *Chakravaka method of Algorithms*: The Chakravaka method is cyclic algorithm to solve in determining quadratic equation including Pell's equation. This method for obtaining integer solutions was developed by Brahmagupta one of the well-known mathematician of 700CE. Another mathematician Jayadurga later generalize this method for a wide range of equations which was further refined by Bhaskara II in his ***Bijaganitha*** Treatise.

(g) *Ruler Measurement*: Excavations at Harappa sites yielded rulers or linear measures made from ivory and shell, marked out in minute subdivisions with an amazing accuracy, the calibrations correspond closely with the hasta increment of 13/8 inches, traditionally used in the ancient architecture of South India. Ancient bricks found at the excavations sites have dimensions that correspond to the units of these rulers.

(h) *A theory of Atom*: One of the notable Scientist of the ancient India was **Kanada** (kanad) who is said to have devised the atomic theory centuries before John Dalton was born. He speculated the existence of ***anu*** (kana) small indestructible in particle, much like an atom. He also stated that once can have to two states absolute rest and the station of motion (proton and electron). He further held that atoms of same substance combined with each other in specific and synchronized manner to reduce *Divyanuka* (diatomic molecules) and ***Tryanuka*** (triatomic Molecules)

(i) *Heliocentric Theory*: Mathematicians of India often applied their mathematical knowledge to make accurate astronomical predictions. The most significant among them was Aryabhatta whose book ***Aryabhattata*** represented the pinnacle of astronomical knowledge at the same time. He correctly propounded that the **Earth, is round, rotates on its own axis and revolves around the Sun** that is the theory heliocentric theory. He also predicted about the Solar System and Lunar and Solar eclipses duration of the day as well as distance between the Earth and Moon.

(j) *Woot Steel*: A pioneering steel alloy matrix developed in India, Woot steel is a crucible steel characterized by the pattern of bands that was now as in the ancient world by many different names such as ***Ukku, Hifwani*** and ***Seri Iron.*** The steel was used to make the famed Damascus swords of Yore that could cleave a falling silk scarf or a block of wood with the same ease. Produced by the Tamils the Chera Dynasty, the first steel of the ancient world was made by ***heating magnetite ore*** in the presence of carbon in a sealed clay crumble kept inside a charcoal furnace.

(k) *Seamless Metal Globe:* Considered one of the most remarkable feats in metallurgy the first seamless celestial globe was made in Kashmir by ***Alikashmiri Ibn Luqman*** in the reign of the Emperor Akbar. In a major feat Metallurgy, Moghul Metallurgists pioneered the method of lost wax casting to make twenty other globe master pieces in the reign of Moghul Empire. Before the globe were discovered in the 1980s. Modern Metallurgists believed that it was technically impossible to ***make metal globe without any seams*** even the in the modern technology.

(l) *Plastic Surgery*: Written by Sushrutha in 6th century BC. ***Sushrutha Samhitha*** is consider to be one of the most comprehensive text book of on ancient surgery. The text mentions various illness plants preparation and use of herbs and cures with complex techniques of plastic surgery. Sushrutha Samhitha's most well-known contribution to plastic surgery is the reconstruction of the nose known as ***rhinoplasty***.

(m) *Cataract surgery*: The first cataract surgery in the world is said to have been performed by the ancient Indian Physician Sushrutha way back in the 6th century BC. To remove the cataract from the eyes, he used a curve needle **Jabamukthi** *salaka* to loosen the lenses and push the cataract out the field of vision. The eye would be bandaged for two days till it is healed completely. Sushrutha surgical works were later translated to Arabic language and through the Arabs, his works were introduced to the West.

(n) *Ayurveda*: Long before the birth of Hippocrates, Charaka, authored a fundamental text, *charakra samhitha* on the ancient science of Ayurveda. Referred to as the father of Indian Medicine, Charaka was the first physician to present the concept of digestion, metabolism and immunity in his book. Charaka's ancient manual on preservative medicine remained a standard work on the subject for millennia and was translated into many foreign languages, including Arabic and Latin.

(o) *Iron cased Rockets*: The first iron cased rockets were developed the 1780's by *Tipu sultan of Mysore* who successfully used the rocket against the larger forces of British East India Company during Anglo-Mysore wars. He crafted long iron tubes filled them with gunpowder and fastened them to bamboo to create the predecessor of the Modern Rocket. With a range of about 2KM these rockets cause damage. Due to them the British suffered of their worst ever defeated in India at the Hands of Tipu.

(p) *Theory of Evolution*: The order of the Dasavatara (10 principle Avatharas) (incarnations) can be interpreted to convey Darwin's evolution. British Genetics and Evolutionary biologist JBS Haldane opined that there are a true sequential of the great unfolding of evolution. Like the evolution process itself, the first avathara of God is Fish-*Matsya*, then comes reptile, *Kurma,* then mammal; the boar **varaha**, then *Narasimha*, a Man-lion being , the dwarf *Vamana,* rest four humans and kalki not yet born. Various thinkers like Helena Bavstky Williams Nabin Chandra, CD Deshmukh have associated the Dasavathara with evolution. In the Sanskrit epic of Hindu mentioned several exotic creatures including ape like humans. Some Hindus see this a proof of the historicity of their mythological character which support the theory of evolution in their texts.

The Ramayana speaks of the ***vanara* an** ape like mammal with human intelligence Caarvaka the Heterodox Philosopher of Vedic time views that creation is cyclic. According to Upanishad the Universe, the Earth along with human creation undergone repeated cycles (pralaya) of creation and destruction. According Hindu cosmology the age of Universe around 4320, 000,000,000 Rig Veda it is suspected the very existence of God only evolution must have caused the birth of Universe and earth. In following Rhyme the Vedic writers clearly specified which include;

> *"Who really knows who can swear*
> *How creation came when or where!*
> *Even Gods came after creation's day*
> *who really knows, who can truly say*
> *when and how did creation start?*
> *Did He do it? Or did He not?*
> *Only He, up these, knows, maybe ;*
> *Or perhaps not even He*
> (Rig Veda 10:1291-7)

Note: The explanation of four human avatars viz. **Parasurama** (stage 6) Forest dweller Humans developed some tools , 7th stage **Rama Hunter;** Humans used with superior weapon which are bows, arrows and created villages; 8th stage **Balarama** farmer the beginning of full-fledged cultivator since bore plough; and finally **Krishna** the 9th stage in which civilized human incarnation and the 10th stage is yet to born that is **Kalki.**

B. Subsequent information available on the Science and Technology through Archaeological survey which speak of the much advanced technology the Vedic Indus valley civilized peoples /seers invented and used which include:

(i) *Iron Pillar of Delhi*: the world's first iron pillar was the Iron Pillar of Delhi erected at the time of Chandra Guptha Vikamadithya (370-413 BCE) The pillar has attracted the attention of Archaeologists and material Scientists have called a "Testament to the Skill of ancient *Black-smithy*" because of high resistance to corrosion.

(ii) *Step Well*: Earliest Clear evidence of the origins of the Step Well in the Indus Valley Civilization's archeological site at Mohenjo-Daro in Pakistan and Dholavira in India. The three features of step well in the subcontinent are evident from one particular site abandoned, a bathing pool, and steps leading down to water and figures of some religious importance into one structure. The early centuries immediately before Common Era saw the Buddhists and Jains of India adapt the step wells into their architecture. Both the Wells and the form of ritual bathing reached other parts of the world with Buddhism.

(iii*) Stupa*: The origin Stupa can be traced to 3rd century BCE. It was used as commemorative monument associated with storing sacred relics. The Stupa architecture was adopted in South East Asia and East Asia, where it evolved into Pagoda.

(iv) *Flush Toilet*: Flush Toilet using water are found in several houses of the cities of Mohenjo-Daro and Harappa from the 3rd millennium BC.

(v) *Plough*: The earliest known instance of a plough field was found at Kaalibagan.

(vi) *Shampoo*: the Shampoo in English is derived from Hinduistani *champoo.* It dates back to 1762. A variety herbs and their extract were used as shampoos since ancient time in India. A very effective early shampoo was made by boiling Sap Indus with dried Indian goose berry (amla) and few other hers using the strained extract. The extract called *ksuma* creates lather which Indian Texts identify as phreak leaves which keep hair soft, shiny and manageable. Gurumukhi the Sikh guru made it referred in as Soap in1600CE.

(vii) *Gravity*: Aryabhatta first identified the force to explain why the objects do not fall when Earth rotates, Brahmagupta, described gravity as an attractive force and used the term

"Guruthvakarshan" for gravity. Aryabhatta developed a geo-centric Solar system of gravitation and eccentric elliptical model of the planets where the planets spin on their axes and follow elliptical orbits the sun and Moon revolved around the Earth.

(viii) *Raman Effect*: the Encyclopedia Britannica (2208) reports "change in wave length of light that occur wherein light beam is deflected by molecules. The Chandrasekhar Venkata Raman, who discovered it in 1928. When a beam of light travel a dust free transparent sample of chemical compound a small fraction of the light emerges in direction other than that of the incident (incoming) beam. Most of this scattered light is of unchanged wavelength. A small part however has wave length different from that of the incident light its presence is a result of "Raman Effect.

(C) Stephen Knapp in his Book Seeing Spiritual India" states the following" India is the sixth largest country in the world, the largest Democracy ever practiced by man on this planet and one of the most ancient and living Civilization will capture her ancient number one place in World as the richest nation and economic giant on earth in the Twenty first Century. Hinduism, Buddhism, Sikhism and Jainism, the indigenous religions of India should to protect India right away with. Without India all these three subsequent religions will fade away.

The late B. R. Ambedkar father of the Indian constitution winner of the prestigious Bharatha Rathna award and great Indian patriot had stated "Given the time and circumstance nothing under the sun shall stop this country from becoming Super power. It is India's fate due to her historical legacy emphasizing compromise, conciliation, cooperation, mutual respect and love, live and let live philosophy to lead the world which is submerged in turmoil, conflict and confrontation. India's culture has spread around the world to her ability to co-exist and synthesize.

Some of the facts about India published in a German Magazine which deals with world History reported in

Publication of Bunts Association of North America (BANA) 1999, California are given below:

- India *never invaded* any country in her last 10,000 years.
- India invented the number system. Zero was invented by Aryabhatta.
- Worlds University was established in Taxila in 700BC
- More 10, 5000 student from all over world studied more than 60 subjects. The University of Nalanda built in the fourth Century BC was one of the greatest achievement ancient India in the field of Education.
- Sanskrit is mother of all the European Language. Sanskrit is the most suitable language for the computer Soft-wear, a report by Forbes Magazine in July 1987.
- Ayurveda is the earliest School of Medicine known to human charka the father medicine consolidated Ayurveda 2500 years ago. Today Ayurveda is fast regaining its rightful place in our civilization.
- The Art of navigation was born in the River 60,000 years ago. The very word navigation is derived from the word **NAVGATH.**
- It is Jagdish Chandra Bose, an Indian Biologist discovered for the first time that there is a life in the plants and trees.
- Algebra, Trigonometry and Calculus came from India. Quadratic equation were used by Sridhar Charya in the 11th Century BC The largest numbers the Greek-roman used were 106 whereas Indians used numbers as big as $10^{**}33$ (10 to the power of 50.
- According to the Gemological Institute of America, up to 1896 India was the *only source of diamonds* to the world.
- USA based IEEE, has proved that has been century old suspension in the world among academics the pioneer of wireless communication Profess Jagdish Bose not Marconi.
- When many cultures were nomadic forest dwellers, over 5000 years ago, India established Harappa culture in Sindh Valley, the Indus Valley Civilization.

- The place of value system, the decimal system was developed in Indian in 100 BCE
- The Value of Pi was first calculated by Bodh Yana and explained the concept of what is now known as the Pythagorean theorem.
- British Scholors in last year (1999) have officially published that Bodh Yana's dates the 6th century is long before European mathematicians.
- The earliest reservoir and dam for Irrigation was in Saurashtra * Sushrutha is the father of surgery. Two thousand six years ago, he and health Scientists of time conducted surgeries like caesarian, cataract, fractures and Urinary stones. Usage of Anesthesia was well known in ancient India.
- Besides this few more important scientific and numerological systems along with theory of Evolution was proposed by Ancient Medieval professionals. And the author of the article Stephen Knapp finally states that "all of the above is just *tip of the iceberg,* the list could be endless".

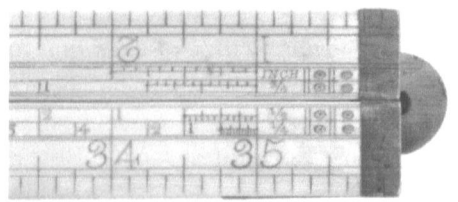

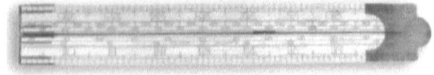

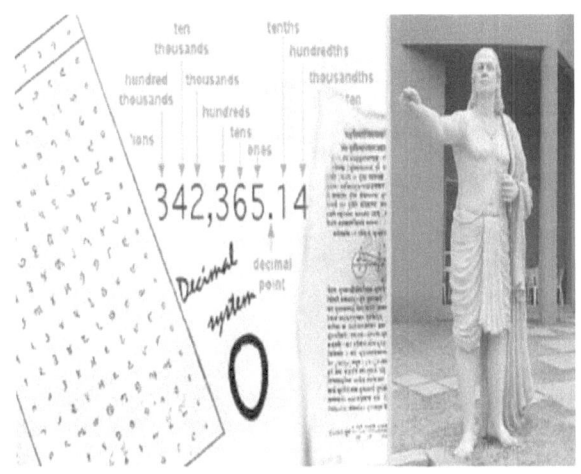

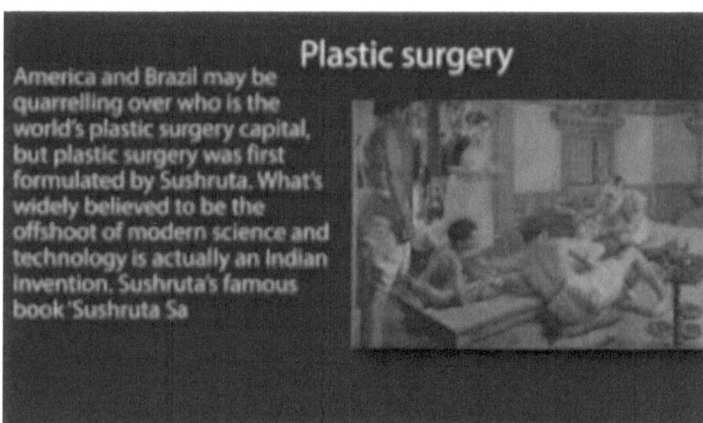

Plastic surgery

America and Brazil may be quarrelling over who is the world's plastic surgery capital, but plastic surgery was first formulated by Sushruta. What's widely believed to be the offshoot of modern science and technology is actually an Indian invention. Sushruta's famous book 'Sushruta Sa

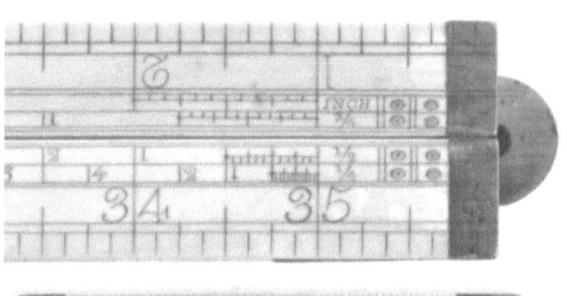

1432 * 12 **IN**
2 **SECONDS ?**

VEDIC MATHS!!!!

$97^2 = 9409$

How?????

$97 = 100 - 3$

$97 - 3 = 94, 3^2 = 09$

$97^2 = 9409$

(D) What others revered Scholars and Philosophers say about our Nation India: a bird eye view report is here under:

(i) Will Durant, An America Historian states that " It is true that even across the Himalayan barrier India has sent to the West, such gifts as grammar, logic philosophy and fables ,hypnotism and chess and above all number and decimal system"

(ii) B.G. Rolle:" Our present knowledge of the nervous system fits in so accurately with the internal description of human body in the Vedas (5000Years ago). Then the question arises whether Vedas are religious books or books of anatomy of the nervous system and medicine."

(iii) Wheeler Wilcox: "India the land of Vedas the remarkable works contain not only religious ideas for a ***perfect life***, but also facts which science has proven true, Electricity, radium, Electronics, Airship, all were known to the seers who founded Vedas.

(iv) Mark Twain: India has two million gods and worships them all. In Religion all other counties are paupers, India is the only millionaire or I must say billionaire"

(iv) (b) "So far as I am able to judge, nothing has left undone either by man or nature, to make the most extraordinary country that the Sun visits on his rounds. Nothing seems to have been forgotten, nothing overlooked"-Mark Twain

(v) Emmalyn Plummet: " India has very advanced Hindu astronomers in 6000 years BCE Vedas contain an account of the dimensions of Earth, Sun Moon planets and Galaxies (Calendars and constellations)

(vi) *Sir William Jones* British Orientalist states that the "Sanskrit language whatever be its antiquity is a wonderful structure, more perfect than the Greek more copious than the Latin and more exquisitely refined than either.

(vii) *Romaine Rollin*, French Philosopher states" If there is one place on the face of Earth where all the dreams of living men have found a home from the very earliest days when man began the dream of existence, it is India"

(viii) *Mac Muller*, German Scholar: " I were asked under what sky the human has most fully developed some of its life and found solutions, I should point to India"

(ix) *Will Durant* An American Historian: India was the mother land of our race and Sanskrit the mother of Europe's language, she was the mother of our philosophy mother through Arabs, of much of our mathematics; mother through the village community of self-government and democracy, mother India is in many ways ***mother of us all***"

(x) P. John Stone : Gravitation was known to the Hindus (Indians) before the birth of Newton. The system of blood circulation was discovered by the centuries before Harvey was the head of"

(xi) Heisenberg, German Scientist states: "After the conversations about Indian Philosophy some of the ideas of Quantum Physics that had a so crazy suddenly made much more sense.

(xii) *Sir W. Hunter* British Surgeon: "The surgery of Ancient India's Physicians was bold and skilful. A special branch of surgery was dedicated to rhinoplasty or operations for improving deformed ears and nose and form in new ones, which Europeans and world surgeons have now borrowed."

(xiii) *William James*, American Author: "From Vedas we learn a practical art of surgery, medicine, music, building under which mechanized are included. They are an encyclopedia of every aspect of life, culture, religion, science, ethics politics, law cosmology and meteorology."

(xiv) *Grant Duff*, British Historian states:" Many of the advances in the Science that we consider today to have been made in Europe were in fact made in India centuries ago"

(xv) *Dr. Arnold Toynbee* a British Historian: "It is already becoming clearer that a chapter which has Western beginning will have an Indian ending of it is not to end self-destruction of human race…At this supremely dangerous movement in History, the only of Salvation for mankind is the *Indian Way*"

(xvi) *Lancelot Hog Ben*: An English Mathematician: There has been no more revolutionary contribution that the one which Hindus (Indian) made when they invented Zero"

(xvii)*Again Max Muller* : There is no book in the world that so thrilling, stirring and inspiring as the Upanishads."

(xviii) *Indian Researcher Ajay Sarma Questions* Albert Einstein's famous mass energy equation " It is only valid under special conditions of the parameters involved example number of light waves, magnitude of light, angels at which waves are emitted with relative velocity. He is an Asst. Director for Education Government of Himachal Pradesh told INS: that " The Equation $E=MC^2$ is inadequate as it has been completely studied and is only valid under special conditions," He further said that "Einstein considered just two light ways of equal energy, emitted in opposite direction and relative velocity uniform. There are numerous possibilities for the parameters which were not considered in Einstein's $E=MC^2$.

I wish that there would be some parallel Universe where India has reached the pinnacle of human cultural and scientific strength and contributed lot more to the global human consciousness as purported above. But I feel there is one fault that has been recurrently in vogue that it has glaringly displayed is domination of English in all the field of education and communication, which may cause damage to our revival attempt. I found that in our country, we have given much importance to English rather than Sanskrit or Hindi and governing authority of India since Independence has not paid attention in implementing the project of Sanskritization in the entire subcontinent. This will help to boost to our attempt of receiving back our lost culture and civilization. Right now we are just English speaking confused people attracted by Western style of living which I feel that it may cause the collapse of the Planet earth in to dooms. Sanskrit and India have been by underrated by the Westerners whose aim is to push down India to the level of slavery as was done earlier by Imperialists and Arab Communalists and this requires another lesson. Like Hebrews got back their country of Israel, we need to struggle to get back our lost glory by boosting through Cultural Revolution by way of non-violence as Gandhi did to get back our cultural Independence. If all Indians, both Hindus and moderate Muslims, Sikhs and Christians it would be like cake walk to achieve back our diamond like culture and civilization. The future ***thought*** makes me feel that Renaissance is in Offing in India. ***And this is certain***.

CHAPTER 3

STRATEGIC INDIAN CULTURE

India's strategic culture is not monolithic, rather Mosaic like, but as a composite is more distinct and coherent that of most contemporary Nation States. This is due to its sustained continuity with the Symbolism of pre-modern Indian State system and threads of Hindu or Vedic civilization dating back several millennia. Embedded in educated, social elites the consciousness Hindu values has been resident in essentially the same territorial space namely the Indian Sub-continent.

This continuity of values was battered and overlaid but never severed or completely submerged, whether by Muslim invasions and Moghul rule the sea-born arrival of French and Portuguese adventures and Missionaries or the encroachment of the British Empire with implantation of representative political Institutions and Modern Law. Indian Culture assimilated much of what we think as 20th century "Modernity"

I begin herewith the propositions on the traits of Indian strategic culture listed in table of I two sections, the first related to the conceptual origin of the traits and the second to their instrumental or behavioral implications. These are dismissed and illustrated later in terms of specific actions and event.

A. Philosophical and Mythological Foundation:

- Sacred parameters of Indian Identity;
- Goals are timeless not time bound;
- India's status is given not earned;
- Knowledge of Truth is the key to action and power;
- World Order is hierarchical, not egalitarianism;

B. Instrumental Implications:

- India's external visage is enigmatic;
- Self-Interest expressed externally is impersonal and absolute;

- Contradictions in the real world are natural and affirmed;
- force has its place but guile may trump force;
- Actions have consequences, good intent does not absolve injury;
- Entitlement inhibits ordinary compromise (hard to split differences, truth is not at ease with quid proquo;
- Compromise easily viewed as internal defeat (ephemeral, bends, truth, dents sovereignty)
- Trust is right knowledge and action is impersonal and hard to build or replenish;
- Security is sedimentary (encompassing a geographic setting and way of life;
- Strategy is assimilative (appearance changes, reality is constant)

Sacred Parameters of Indian Identity:

Indian strategic culture has a collective consciousness of the sacred origins of Indian-ness that give mythological and metaphysical significance to the sub-continent as a terrestrial expression. Great rivers symbolize life-giving and cleansing properties of the material world and connect mortal's god and to underlying cosmic forces (after Ganga, Goddess and Purification) is dotted with places of pilgrimage and temples from its source in the Himalayas and Bay of Bengal. India's natural (spiritual) frontier begins in the Himalayas where the great rivers rise and follows to where they join the sea.

Mark Twain in his appreciation of Indian culture states that "India is the cradle of human race, the birth place of *human speech*, the mother of history, the grandmother of Legends and great grandmother of tradition. Our most valuable and most instructive materials in the history of man are treasure up in India only" As booster of India's appreciation, Max Muller, German scholar styles India by stating that "If I were asked under what sky the human mind has most fully developed some of its choicest gifts, has most deeply pondered on the greatest of life and has found solution, I should point India". That is our India's Incredibility. That is the acknowledgement we can render to our India's culture. Our India and our India's culture has an extraordinary impact over world civilizations.

The culture of India refers collectively to the thousands of distinct and unique cultures of all religions and communities present in India. India's language, religion, dances, music, architecture, food differs from place to within country. The Indian culture labeled as an amalgamation of several cultures, spans across the Indian subcontinent and has been influence by history that is several millennia old. Many elements of India's culture, such as Indian Religions, Indian Philosophy and Indian culture, have a profound impact across the world.

"A man reaps what he sows" and the Philosophy, culture and Religion of Indian Hinduism. According to Hinduism every deed that has ever been performed produces its fruit and the doer much eat the fruits. This means every action that we perform in life, every word we speak and even every thought we think has its reaction. In the *classic Hinduism actions (Karma) and Duty (Dharma) were the dominant concepts Karma* as the accumulations of good and bad actions would influence a person's destiny.

(A) Spiritual Freedom: For thousands of centuries, India's great seers have expounded spiritual wisdom from what is widely believed to be the World's oldest religion. When exploring the iconic Hindu texts and teaching of immortalized Sadhus, it became clear to see that two of these most important truths that *Karma* and *Dharma* or action and duty. In fact, because these two terms have been relevant across India's holy lands since ancient times, the country of other great religions of Buddhism and Jainism and Sikhism which were usually influenced by Hinduism, have incorporate them to their own theologies albeit with slightly different meaning. Yet still it is certain that the roots of these great spiritual concept trace back to the Hindu scriptures and it is there we can turn out our attention to gain understanding of laws *of Karma and Dharma*.

Hinduism is not a religion but rather a family of religions. And that the culture of Indian civilization. There is no single leader who has been identified as the founder of Hindu ism. It is thought have gotten its name from Persian Hindu/Sindh meaning river, used by outsiders to describe the people of the Indus River valley. Later Muslim invaders called the religion Hinduism, the country of the people of Hind/Sind. In 18th and 19th centuries the term Hindu was coined to describe the religions, customs culture and way of life of the people of India. The History of Hinduism can be divided into four periods:

1. Indus Valley Civilization.
2. Vedic Period
3. Philosophical and
4. Bhakti.

HINDU LOVE PEACE AND SECULAR AND EXISTENCE:

Hindus believe that all living creatures from worm to blue whale, from monkey to man, sprout to Sherman, flora to fauna, wee bill to ostrich, and pebble to sandstone and water to wind have souls which are essentially equal and these life forms are manifestation of the Unity of Universe. This is most of the Hindus are vegetarian and abhor killing animals and ahimsa, the belief that it is a sin to harm any living creatures is an important percept in Hindu thought. The concept was eluded in the Upanishads and contrasts sharply with doctrines of western religion which holds that mankind is a special creation on a plane higher than creatures. Thus human being meaning of life (Purusharthan) named ***dharma, artha, Kama and Moksha***.

Concept of Salvation: To attain Moksha (salvation) is the aim of life in Hindu society. In Hinduism. In Hindu culture there are two words for soul. Brahman is the world soul and Atman is the individual soul. The Hindu's ultimate goal is for individual to be ultimately united with one encompassing World soul Brahman, like rain drop falling to the ocean. Until the unity occurs the individual soul is born from time after time. Salvation in

Hinduism therefore is not the forgiveness of sin committed against god. Contrariwise salvation is quest to end all earthy suffering an escape of from illusion and successful attainment of Nirvana (*salvation)* and Salvation can be attained through three general ways:

1. **Karma Marga** – It is the way of works of performing cast duties scrupulously.

2. **Gnana Marga**: It is the way of knowledge using the intellect man has to study the Vedas and attains his wisdom from the sacred texts.

3. **Bhakti Marga**: It is the way of love and devotion to Gods.

Karma Marga is the most popular way of salvation in the world. So below the research is going to do deep study on Karma and its relation to Dharma.

B Theory Karma in Hinduism (definition and meaning) of Karma. Karma originally meant ritual act precisely performed to produce power. It is derived from the Sanskrit root Kar –'to do' and signifies literally 'what is done' a deed. Karma literally means 'work' or action but also indicates the consequences of action is within existence which flow into the next existence and influence its character and so the chain goes on. Karma is also the moral law of cause and effects wherein an individual is given precisely what he has earned"

The Origin of Karma: the source of the doctrine of Karma lies hidden in the history of the people of the Indian subcontinent. Although the theory of rebirths does not appear in the Vedas there is evidence that the people of this period believed that there ritual actions had consequences for those who had died. Several theories have been proposed as to how the doctrine may have emerged from the concepts found in the Vedas. It is written in Vedas that the deeds of the dead are weighed in the balance. The dead are then rewarded or punished in accordance with the appropriateness' of their derivation at all, but was incorporated from the religion of the indigenous people. The concept of births was part of the religion of the tribes of the Ganges Region.

(a) Purpose of Karma is to lead man from his ineluctable bondage to liberation;

(b) Karma is meant to teach lessons. If we learn quickly we will make progress towards perfection;

(c) The law of Karma makes righteous living;

(d) The effects of the earlier deed cannot be wiped out;

(e) The consequences of Karma within Hinduism the effect of Karma leads to the caste system;

(f) Lack of inner Peace people know that it is caused by karma;

(g) Bad karma brings bad future and good karma being good actions. The law of karma operates by itself. No god can interfere with this law.

The theory of Karma is referred in all the Scriptures of Hinduism. The term Karma are found copiously occurs almost *40 times* in the *Rig-Veda* but never in the sense of the theories on transmigration. It means simply, works, deed and especially sacred actions. Karma directly related to the central idea of sacrifice. Later it was miss-interpreted. There is no doubt that every being including gods and celestial beings are bound by the law of karma.

Secondly there is reference of Karma theory in Upanishad wherein it defines that as *one believes so does the he come*. The doer of good become good and the doer of evil karma becomes evil (Brhadaranya Upanishad chapter 4 Verse 5).

Thirdly In the Bhagavad –Gita there is an entire chapter with the subject of Karma. He who is free from attachment, who is liberated whose mind is established in the knowledge whose actions are but action of sacrifice, his actions are completely dissolved. His offering is Brahman, his oblations is Brahman, and his sacrifice is for Brahman. Thus he certainly attain Brahman who finds Brahman situated in all activities (Bhagavad-Gita: Chapter 4, 23, 24)

(C) The Theory of Dharma: The hierarchy of caste was depicted as built into the order of creation. The Law of Manu chapter 1. 93 stated as "As the Brahman sprang from Brahmas mouth, as he was the first born and possession the Vedas by the right the month as he was the first born and possess the Veda he is by the right of the Lord of this whole creation. From arms the Kshatriya, from his thigh Vaishya and from his feet Sudra. The Brahmans were associated with white the color of purity and lightness, the Kshatriyas with red, the color of Passion and energy, the Vaishya with yellow the color of earth and Sudra with black the color of darkness and inertia.

(D) The connection of Dharma and Karma: Karma is thus inseparable from Dharma and samsara. "One is born in certain caste is an outcome of one's born past deeds in an earlier in connections. It means Dharma is his life's dispensation based on his past karma. A man whether is he in Brahmans, Kshatriya Vaishya or Sudra is such by nature. By evil deeds twice-born man falls from his position. Continuous bad karma results in rebirth into lower life forms. The Kshatriya, Vaishya who lives in condition of Brahman who having attained the Brahman-hood which is so hard to get, follows the profession of Vaishya, under the influence of cupidity and delusion, fall into the condition of Vaishya. A Brahman who fall from his own duty becomes after wards a Sudra by practicing good works , a Sudra becomes a Brahman

SECTION II TREATISE ON SAMSARA (Human life)

Samsara is a Sanskrit word meaning "to wander" or "to flow" through and is recognized with the Hindu religions as the continuous cycle of death and rebirth. Samsara is the result of one's Karmic actions and thought throughout their present and pre-existing life times. Samsara can also be seen as the ignorance of atman (true self) and absolute reality (Brahman). Wen realizing atman one can then attain Moksha (liberation). Moksha is seen as the highest achievement that any being can accomplish and inevitable leads to ending Samsara. Samsara can also betide to or known as worldly Existence. It is the constant altering station continuous wheel which never ends nor begins.

The Jiva and Jivatma (Soul) is that which travel continuously through birth and death carrying with its karmic residue. The Jiva is reborn (Punarjanma) into various different realms and beings; the realms widely accepted. One can be born into a heaven, hell or earthly existence. Depending on the karmic nature of a Jiva it can be reborn as an insect, animal, plant, human beings, and different Vargas (caste) of human being and finally god in any of three realms. The human form is one of the rarest that one can be reborn into and although it is one of the more desirable forms. It is Moksha which is ultimate attainment which stops the process of being reborn.

One's dharma also interwoven with Karma and subsequently entwined with Samsara. A King's dharmic action is in direct relation to the wellbeing of himself and his kingdom. However if he were to neglect his dharmic duties then his next life may be lower in the caste system or even as a lower life form as discussed in above sections.

Kama (sensory pleasure) also plays an integral part of in Samsara as action can be shaped as Karma. Kama within the Hindu tradition is a part of the mind which feeds the body. Kama can also be defined as "desire" and desires' born in the mind that influences the actions of body. When Jiva has been rid of desire (**Kama**) and worldly pleasures *bhukti* can also keep them with samsara. The Upanishad say that one's desire for life and its trivial matter can cause the soul constantly reborn again and again into suffering of the world until its desires for life and world ceases.

The Hindu view of life within *samsara* as a repetition of the re-death and re-birth were present within the ancient traditions before samsara was named and both are continuously associated with fear. The Jiva is immortal, however its bodies must continuously die and be reborn into lives filled with threat of fear or hunger and the pain of sorrow and hardships such as old age, or diseases in seemingly endless cycle. The body tied to samsara until it can realize its "self". The 'ignorance' of atman is called 'avidya' and this ***avidya*** could be equated to a veil; it is the Jiva supposed perception of itself and its own limitations. Theory suggest that the true nature of one's soul is hidden from it. Because Samsara. Once ***the veil*** is removed it is possible for the Jiva to realize Atman. It is at this point Buddhism and Jainism takes the inspiration and proposed their own theory deviating certain ways and means to establish their own theory.

Thus *Samsara* is viewed as an eternal wheel continues without beginning or end and through Moksha is seen as liberation from that eternal when, there are those who are seen to accept their position within the ***cyclic samsara***. Though samsara is viewed as painful repetition process there or those who would aspire to gain the Vargas (caste) without moksha. That is why followers practice a more pious and charitable lifestyle seeking not end *samsara* but instead to ensure a better birth in their next life following their present life time.

To conclude it need to be discussed that according to Hinduism Man is the maker of his own destiny. Here never God interfere with is karma and his destiny. One becomes good and by doing good actions and bad by bad actions while executing and discharging his duties of samsara. The evolving process of life and death continue until Mukti is attained by good deeds. But with Karma man has to follow dharma which means he has to work according the caste and stages of life. Today still these teaching are familiar in Hinduism and caste system is still an integral part of the social order, even though it has been outlawed by the Indian government.

There is no reincarnation at all. Good works are important to do but no as a way to get salvation. The Bible tells that Salvation can only be received as a gift from God and cannot be earned in any way. The gift of salvation is given to us argues Jesus Christ.

Theory of Dharma and Karma and finally quitting of Samsara through Karmic method, though look logically unacceptable but one should appreciate the Hindu thought was so matured without the infrastructure of Telescope and experiments of nuclei which is a power that the caused the life. The Classical and most profound trans of philosophy that

resembles the theory of cosmology promulgated by modern Science underscored by Philosophy which is almost nearer to the ***truth of the birth of universe***. The Nucleolus can be termed as Brahman (***paramatma***) the chain of birth and death under the ambit of inexplicit and in cognizable Power the Nuclei has caused the Big Bang and out of which the entire Universe is tend to operate without rest and without break. The Western Monotheistic religions which called (Scientific thought) contrary to Hindu thought, have invented the Icons like Yahweh/ Lord God/Allah who is said to be the Creator and caused the creation which is illogical and irrelevant and which cannot accepted in any core.

CHAPTER 4

SPICE TRADE

"When it is a matter of opinion, I make my opinion matter"

The spice trade refers to the trade between historical civilizations in Asia, North East Africa and Europe spices such as cinnamon cassia, cardamom, ginger pepper and turmeric were well known and used in antique for commerce in the Eastern world.

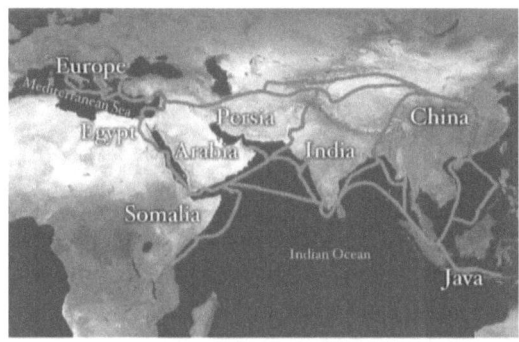

The spice trade from India attracted the attention of the Ptolemaic dynasty, and subsequently the Roman empire

Dutch ships in Table Bay docking at the
Cape Colony at the Cape of Good Hope,
1762

Opium was a part of the spice trade driven by Opium addition. These spices found their way in the Middle East before the beginning of the Christian era where the source of these spices were withheld by the traders and associated with fanatic tales. Early writings and Stone Age carving of Neolithic age obtained indicates that India's South Coastal port **MUZRI** in Kerala had established itself as a major spice trade center from as early as 3000 BC which marked the beginning of the spice trade. Kerala, referred as the land of spices or **"Spice Garden of India"** was the place traders and explores wanted to reach including Christopher Columbus, Vasco Da Gama and others. The Greco Roman world followed by trading along the **"Incense route"** and the Roman. India Route during the first millennium during the first millennium, the Sea route and Sri Lanka (The Roman–Taprobane) controlled by the Sea. The Kingdom of the Axum 5rh Century BCE and11AD had pioneered The Red Sea route before the 1st century and Mid7th Century AD after the rise of Islam Arab Traders started dominating the maritime routes. Arab Traders started dominating the maritime ranks. Arab Traders eventually took over the conveying goods via the Levant and venation merchants to Europe until the rise of Ottoman Turks, cut the route to again by 1453. Overland routes helped the spice trading emporiums throughout the Indian Ocean, tapping source regions in East Asia and Shipping spices trading emporiums in India West Ward to Persian Gulf and the Red Sea, from which overland routes led to Europe.

The trade rout was changed by the European Ages of Discovery, during which spice trade, particularly in black pepper, became influential activity for European traders. The cape route from Europe to the Indian ocean via Cape of Good Hope" was pioneered by the Portuguese Pepper, became an influential activity for European traders. The Cape route in Europe from Europe to the Indian Ocean via the Cape of Good Hope was pioneered by Portuguese Explorer, Navigator Vasco Da Gama in 1450 resulting in new maritime routes for trade. This trade- diving the world economy from the end of the middle ages well into the Modern times, ushered in an age of European and Arab Domination in the East. Channels such as Bay of Bengal served as a bridge for cultural and commercial exchanges between diverse cultures as nation's struggled to gain control of the trade along with many spice. Europeans, in particular, who notorious in maritime on sea routes. Europeans domination was slow to develop. Portuguese trade route were mainly restricted and limited by the use of ancient routes, Ports, and Nations that were difficult to dominate. The Dutch were later able to bypass many of these problems by pioneering a direct ocean route from the Cape Good Hope and the Sunda Straight in Indonesia.

Origin:

The Egyptians had traded in the Red Sea, spices from 'Land of Punt' and from Arabia. Luxury goods traded along the Incense Route included Indian, spices, and ebony (Timber), silk and fine textiles. The spice trade was associated with overland routes early as but maritime routes proved to be the factor which helped the trade grow. The Polemic Dynasty, had developed trade with India using the Red Sea Ports.

People from Neolithic period in spices, obsidian (raw dark glass), sea shells, precious stones and other high value materials, as early as the 10 Millennium BC. In the first millennium the Arabs, Phoenicians and Indians were engaged in sea trade, in luxury goods such as spices, gold, precious stones, leather of rare animal's ebony and pearls. The sea trade was in the Red Sea route in the Rea Sea from Bab-el-Mandeb to Berenice from there by land to the Nile and then by boats to Alexandria. The land trade was in Catamaran boats and sailing with the help of the Waterlines in the Indian Ocean.

In the second half of the millennium BC the Arab tribes of South and West Arabia took control over the land trade of spices from South Arabia to the Mediterranean Sea. The tribes were the main Quataban, Hadhamout, Saba and Himaril. In the north the Nabataea's took control of the trade route that crossed the Niger from Petra to Gaza. The trade made the Arab tribes very rich. The South Arabia region was called Eudemon (elated) Arabia by the Greeks and was on the ***agenda of conquests of Alexander of Macedonia before he died***. The Indians and Greeks had control over the sea trade. In the late second century BC the Greeks from Egypt learned from Indians how to sail directly from Aden to the West coast of India using the monsoon winds (Hippalus) and took control over the sea trade.

Arabian and Medieval Europe: From the time immemorial South Arabia (Arabia Felix antiquity) had been a trading center for frankincense, myrrh and other fragrant resins and gums. Arab traders artfully withheld the true sources of the spice they sold. To satisfy their Market artfully withheld the true sources ***they spread fanatic tales to the effect that cassia grew in shallow lakes guarded by winged animals and the cinnamon in deep glens infested with poisonous snakes.*** But Piney Elder (AD 23-70) ridiculed the stories and boldly declared that "all these have been... evidently invented for the purpose of enhancing the price of these commodities." The spice trade had brought great riches to the Abbasid, Caliphate and even inspired famous legends as that of Sindbad the Sailor. The India commercial connection with East Asia proved vital to the merchants of Arab and Persia during 7th and 8th Centuries.

All though the origins of spices were known thorough Europe by the middle ages, no ruler proved capable of breaking the Venetian hold on the trade routes near the end of the 15th Century. However explorer began to build ships and venture abroad in search of new ways to reach spice, producing regions. So began the famed voyages of discovery. 1492 Christopher Columbus sailed under the flag of Spain, 1497 John Cabot, on behalf of England, but both failed to find the storied spices lands. Under the command of a Portuguese was the first European to bring spices from India. Europe by way of Cape Good Hope in 1501. Portuguese went to dominate the naval trading route through much of the 16th century.

In 1577 English Admiral Francis Drake began his voyage around the world by way of the Strait of Magellan and Spice Island, ultimately sailing the Golden Hind, heavily landed with cloves from Ternate Island in to its home port of Plymouth in 1580. For Holland, a fleet under the command of Cornelius De Houtman sailed for the spice islands in 1595, Jacob Van Eck put sea in 1598 both returned home with rich cargoes of cloves, mace, nutmeg and black pepper,. This success laid the foundation for the prosperous Dutch East India Company formed in 1602.

Similarly, the French East India Company was organized in 1664 by State authorization under Luis XIV. Other East India companies charted by European countries met the varying success. In subsequent struggles to gain control of the trade, Portugal eventually eclipsed, after more than a century as dominant power. By the 19th century British interests were firmly rooted in India and Ceylon, while Dutch were control of the greater part of the East Indies.

It is the naked truth that Westerns including Arabs learned navigation from Indians but they have back stabbed the innocent India and drew an agenda of coquetting it by way of ***Incenses Sea Route and Silk Road, the land route*** and started invading India and netted it like golden fish. This Trade lead to inauguration of laying foundation stone to cause for effecting India to get looted it's treasure of Gold and diamonds and mineral wealth including manpower (as slaves) which further caused annihilation of people living in India, along with heritage of its rich legacy of Vedic knowledge. How and when the ground was prepared to torment the very civilization into pieces and make their intention of colonization implemented in India, the ensuing sections would speak. The First Holocaust in the world on Hindus Buddhists and Jains. Hindu Kush mountain range painted with Hindu blood by the invaders of Europeans and Arabs in the name of missionary is one of the standing example of the so called Holocaust in the name of *Kefir* (Idolaters).

CHAPTER 5

SPICE TRADERS AND MISSIONARY INVASIONS ON INDIA

For more than two Millennia, Golden Hind suffered one bloody invasion after invasion, leaving Holocaust of millions of lives and civilizations and culture left in ruins. Though ours is a country only one of the great ancient civilizations that has survived till today, and Hinduism is most ancient and only continuously surviving religion, many foreigners who knew the India is rich by running its rich spices into trade, had developed jealous of it and started invading one after another. The first of the major invasions came from Alexander of Macedonia. His invasion of India was intended to bring Greek culture to India and encourage cultural exchange between the Indic Hellenic worlds. This invasion was mild compared to the savage invasions of Islam, which continue even today attempt in to dominate the Indian religions of Dharma and the culture of Bharathvarsha.

The contemporary, French writer Franco Gautier has said" the Massacres perpetuated by Muslims in India are unpatrolled in History, bigger than the Holocaust of Jews by the Nazis or massacre of the Armenians by the Turks, more extensive even than the slaughter of the South American native population invading Spanish and Portuguese. Just as India about to successfully throw the yoke of Islamic Barbarianism after nearly 1000 years of slaughter, the British and Portuguese came with business of spices and their missionary mind. They tried to finish years what Islam had begun, beginning of centuries more colonial strangulation of the Vedic culture of India, until finally India won the Independence in 1947. By then so *much damage had been done that India was forced to accept partition along religious lines and give up much of her northern territories* to what are today the Islamic states of Pakistan and after 25 year Bangladesh was portioned in 1971.

What is left of modern India is still rife with growing population of Muslims and continuing threat of Christian Missionaries only seeking to wipe out Hindu, which is not only the majority religion in India, but more than that the India way of life and her very culture. Here I present a brief overview of the history of the foreign invasions and occupations of India.

1. Alexander invasion (336-323 BCE)

Alexander was the King of Macedonia, a nation north of the city States of ancient Greece which was heavily influenced by the Hellenic (Greek) culture. Alexander was the obedient student of Greatest Philosopher, Aristotle, who is promulgated not only philosophy but designed the science. He is called *"father of Science"*. When Alexander was 21 old, in the year 336, when he decided to invade India after having conquered much of Asia Minor and Middle East. A great battle was fought. For the first time the Greeks met elephants in war. The huge beasts were very terrible to look upon. Their awe full trumpeting made the Greek horses sheer and tremble. Most of the Indian believe that, Alexander soldiers were far better drilled and far stronger than the Indians. His horseman changed the elephants in flank and they stung to madness by Greek darts turned to flee. Trampling many of the soldiers of Porus to death in their fright. The Indian war chariots stuck fast in the mud, Porus himself was wounded. Although he yielded to the conqueror. *This was how the Europeans drafted in the History of India.*

But according to new study, Marshall Zhukov documented that, a formidable army led by Alexander of Macedon invaded India. He came from Macedonia whose army comprised with Macedonian soldiers, Balkan fighters and Persian allies. The total numbered more than 41000. Their more memorable clash was at the Battle of HydasIn reality, Zhuko'spea (Jhelum) against the army of Porus, the ruler of the Pourava Kingdom of Western Punjab. For more than 25 centuries it was believed that Alexander forces defeated the Indian Greek and Roman account say the Indians were bested by the superior courage and stature of the Macedonians.

In reality, Zhukov's viewed that "Alexander had suffered a great set back in India than Napoleon in Russia". He further stated that "***The Assakenoi offered stubborn resistance from the mountain strong hold of Massaga, Bazira and Ora. According to Greek sources for several days the armies eyeballed each other across the river. The Greek-Macedonian force after having lost several thousand soldiers fighting the Indian Mountain cities were terrified at the prospect of fierce Pourava army. They had about the havoc Indian war elephants among enemy ranks. The modern equivalent of battle tanks, the elephants also scared with out of the crisis in the Greek cavalry. Another terrible weapon in the Indian's armory was two meter bow. As tall as man could launch massive arrows to transfix more than one enemy soldier.***

Indian strike: The battle was savagely fought. In the first charge by the Indians, Porus's brother Amarsing Killed Alexander's favorite horse Bucephalus forcing Alexander to dismount. This was big deal. In battles outside India the elite Macedonian guards had not allowed a single soldier deliver so much as a search on their King's body, let alone slay his mount. Yet in the battle Indian troops not only broke into Alexander's Inner cardoon, they also killed Nicaea of his leading commander. According to the Roman historian Marcus Justine Porus challenged, who charged him on horseback. In ensuing dual, Alexander fell off his horse and was at the mercy of the Indian Kings' spear. But Porus dithered for second and Alexander's body guards rushed into save their King.

Plutarch, the Greek Historian and biographer say "there seem to have been nothing wrong with Indian morale. Despite the setbacks, when their vaunted Chariots got stuck in mud, Porus Army "rallied and kept resisting the Macedonians with unpassable bravery."

Although the Greeks claim victory the financial resistance put by the Indian Soldiers and ordinary people everywhere had shaken the nerves of Alexander's army to the core. They refused to move further. ***Nothing Alexander could say or do would spur his men to continue east ward. The army was close to a mutiny***

Plutarch says "The combat with Porus took the edge off the Macedonians courage and stayed their further progress into India. For having found it hard enough to defeat an enemy who brought but 20,000 foot and 2000 horses in the field, they fought they had reason to oppose Alexander's design of leading men to pass the Ganges on the further side which was covered with multitude of enemies." Hundred Kilometers from the Indian heartland, Alexander ordered a retreat which made soldiers to become jubilant among his army. Thus the above retrieval of History speaks that the Indian King defeated Alexander and instead of killing him he allowed to back to Greek for any further attempt.

It is all the twisted tactics played by the British rulers who documented the events of History of India. ***Though Alexander was actually defeated by Porus British Historians recorded the event as the Alexander defeated Porus and released him on compassionate grounds. But actually it is the Porus who exonerated and advised him go back to his home, as his beloved horse was killed and Alexander was suffering with irrecoverable wounds.*** The reason for representing Indian history, was out of affinity of that Alexander belongs to their region called Europe.

2.The Arab Invasions: 636 CER-850 CE:

While regularly tasting Indian ***Spice and satisfying their carnal desire***, the Arabs got prepared to invade India both to loot wealth and women by converting or killing infidels of India. In terms Religion, every Mohammedan is destined either convert non-Muslims and kill if not converted and this is called Devine Duty of every Muslim, be it is an ordinary commoner or King or emperor. In Muslim Hadith (Bukhari) prophet Muhammad has quoted by saying that "Two groups of my Ummah, Allah has protected from the hell (FIRE) a group that will conquer India; a group that will be with Isa Ibn Mariayam (Jesus son of Mary). "The first attempted invasion of India by Muslim occurred in 636 CE under Caliph Umar within four years of Muhammad's death. The first 16 invasions attempts utterly failed. But the 17th attempt to invade India by Muhammad bin- Qasim, which was carried out against the wishes of Caliphate, was successful. Qasim marched with 15000 men. He arrived at Debal a port city near the modern Karachi (Pakistan), 711CE. Then he has bolstered by the arrival of his artillery by Sea route (Incense rout) and took the town. This was followed by his conquests of Aror, located north of Hyderabad (Pakistan) in June 712. In the fighting before Aror, the Raja Dahir was slain. In the next year also he conquered the important city of Multan. When an Arab Governor of Sindh Junaid, sought to seize Kachch and Malwa, he was foiled by the pratihara and Gurjara Kings. The Arabs thus unable to expand beyond Sindh but they were able to maintain their hold on Province. In 985 CE Ismail Fatamid dynasty declared its Independence in Multan?

There are three most important of the Raj Put states in North India were the Gahwals of Kanouj, the Paramaras of Malwa and the Chouhans of Ajmer and besides these number of smaller dynasties in different parts of the country such as the Kalachuris in the area around Jabalpur, the Chandselas in Bundelkhand, the Chalukyas of Gujarat the Tomar of Delhi, Bengal remained under the control of the Palas and later Senas. Most of the Rajput rulers of the time were champions of Hinduism, some Jainism's, the Rajput Rulers protected the privileges of Brahmans, and of the caste system in the tenth and twelfth century, temples building activity in North India reached its climax ,there was an internal continuous struggle and warfare between Rajput States. And this was the right occasion to invade India by Turks.

Mohammad Gazhni raided in 1000ADwith his first victory against Hindu Kings of Peshawar. In a short period of 25 years, he is said to have made 17 raids into India. Secondly his most daring raids were against Kanauj in 1018 and against fabulously rich Somanatha Temple of Gujarat.

Mahmud of Ghuri: The second Turkish attack was led by Muizzu'd-Din in 1182. He initially conquered Sindh and Lahore, but to his dismay, he was conquered by Pruthvi Raj Chauhan the first battle at Tarain in 1191. Subsequently, in the battle of Tarain in 1192, Chauhan was defeated and the Kingdom of Delhi fell to Muhammad Ghuri. Before Ghuri's assassination in 1206 Turkish control had been established along with whole length of Ganga, Bihar, and Bengal were also over run. However Ghuri's conquest started a new era in Indian history that is the ***Delhi Sultanate***.

The Mamluk (slave) Dynasty 1206-1290 CE: The Ghuri's Conquest became the nucleus of a new political entity of India-the Delhi Sultanate. For almost 100 years after the Delhi Sultanate was involve in foreign internal conflicts among the Turkish leaders and the dispossessed Raj Put Rulers and Chiefs to regain their Independence. Ghuri left his Indian possessions in the care of his former ***slave, General Qutb-u-din Aibak***. He played an important part in expansion of the Turkish sultanate in India after the battle of Terrain. On the death of his master, Aibak severed his links with Ghazni and asserted his ***independence and founded the Slave Dynasty (Mamulks)***. He helped to prevent India being drawn into central Asian politics and enabled the Delhi Sultanate to develop independently.

Iltumush (1210-1236) succeeded Aibak as the Sultan by defeating Aibak's son. Thus the ***Principle of heredity of son*** succeeding his father was checked at the outset.

Iltumush must be regarded as the real consolidator of the Turkish conquests in North India. He gave new Capital, Delhi a monarchical form of government. He introduced Iqta-grant or revenue from a territory in lieu of salary. He remained a central Army and introduced coins of Tanka (silver) and Jital (copper). The famous Qutub Minar was completed during his reign. He dispatched an expenditure against the Chalukyas of Gujarat but it was repelled with losses.

Just around this time, Mongols under the leadership of Genghis khan, swept across Central Asia and mercilessly sacked the Kingdoms. They periodically crossed river Indus to attack Punjab and Iltumush had to keep constant check on this side. During his last years Iltumush finally nominated his daughter *Razia* (1236-1239) to the throne. *Razia was the first and only Muslim lady to sit on the Delhi throne*. In order to assert her claim, Razia had to contend against her brother as well as against powerful Turkish nobles, and could rule only for three years.

Though brief, her rule had a number of interesting features like the beginning of the struggle for power between the Monarchy and the Turks chiefs, sometimes called as *forty or Chahalgami*. She successfully established law and order in the length and breadth of her Kingdom. In 1239 Ad an internal rebellion broke out which Razia was imprisoned and killed by bandits. The struggle between the Monarchy and the Turkish Chiefs continued till one of the Turkish Chiefs Balban (Ulug Khan) 1265-1285, ascended the Throne during the earlier period he held the position of Naib, Deputy to Nasiruddin Mahamud, a younger son of Iltumush. He broke the Chahalgami and made the Sultan all important. After Balban death there was again confusion in Delhi for some times. In 1290 the Khiljis under the leadership of Jalaluddin Khilji wrested power from the incompetent successor of Balban.

The Khiljis (1290-1320): The Khilji used their Afghan descent to win the loyalties of the discontented nobles, who felt they had been neglected by earlier Slave. Sultan Jalauddin Khilji tried to migrate some of the harsh aspect of Balban's rule. He was the first ruler to put forward the view that the state should be based on the willing support of the governed and that since the majority of Indian were Hindu the state cannot be truly Islamic.

(i) Allauddin Khilji (1296-1316) treacherously murdered his uncle and father- in-law in relation. But harsh methods, he cowed down the nobles and subservient to the crown. He was ambitious and *dreamt of an all India Empire*. During his 25 years tenure, he brought Malwa, Gujarat and Rajasthan under his control. To solve the water problems in summer he constructed lot of Bowlis (wells). His famous general Malik Kabur led the campaign (1308-1312) to the South and defeated Yadav's of Deogiri, the Kakatiyas of Warangal and Hoysalas of Dwarsamudra. Allauddin also repelled the Mongols successfully. His military standing army directly recruited and paid by the State. He revoked all grants made by previous Sultans, introduced *price control*, covering almost the entire market and rationed the grain. In order to effectively subordinate nobles he banned drinking intoxicants. The Sultan permission was necessary before marriage could be arranged among the members of nobility, so that marriage alliances of Political nature could be prevented. No further Rebellion took place during his life time, but in the long run his methods proved harmful to the dynasty.

In 1334 bubonic plaque upped out more than half of his army and it ceased to be effective. Due to this in 1334 the Pandyan Kingdom (Madurai) rejected the authority of the Sultanate and this was followed by Warangal, the Kakatiyas. In 1336 the Vijayanagar Empire and in 1337 Bahamani kingdom were founded that built magnificent capital cities with many building, promoted arts also provided law and order and the development of commerce and handicrafts. Thus while the forces disintegration gradually triumphed in North India, South India and the Deccan had a long spell of stable government.

(ii) Firozsha Tughlaq (1351): Firozsha Tughlaq succeeded Muhammad Having become Sultan with the support of the Nobles and theologians, he had to appease them. His death was followed by civil war among his decedents. The Sultanate became weak and in 1398 the Mongols under the leadership of Timor mercilessly sacked and plundered Delhi. Timor returned to central Asia leaving his nominee to rule the Punjab.

The Sayyid and Lodi Dynasties:

The Tughlaq Dynasty ended soon after the invasion but the Sultanate survived, though it was merely a shadow of its former self. Timor nominee captured Delhi and was proclaimed the new Sultan and Sayyid Dynasty (1414-1451) which was true to rule the earlier half of the century the fifteenth century. But their rule was short lived and confined to a radius of some 200 miles around Delhi. They kept the machinery going until a more capable dynasty, the Lodi's took over. The Lodi's were pure Afghan origin and brought an eclipse to the Turkish nobility. Bahlul Lodi established in Punjab after the Timor's invasion. The most important Lodi Sultan was Sikandar Lodi (1489-1517) who controlled Ganga valley as far as the Bengal. He moved his capital from Delhi, to be able to control the Kingdom better to a new town which later became famous as the *City of Agra.* The last Lodi Ibrahim asserted his absolute power and did not considered the tribal feelings. This lead to his making enemies with them. Finally they plotted with Babar and succeeded in over throwing him in 1526 at the first battle of Panipat. As the power of Sultanate declined, a number of other Kingdoms arose.

In the Western India	The Malwa and Gujarat
In the Eastern India	Jaunpur and Bengal
In the Northern India	Kashmir
In the Southern India	The Vijayanagar and Bahamani

As the Islamic population in India swelled, on account of forced conversions the identity of the Indian Moslem acquired a definition. Islam now actively influenced, most facets of life. The most of Hindus adopted Purda system (veiling) and their language began to be written in Arabic system, leading to *new language called Urdu*. The calligraphy came into its own and was raised to the highest form of imposition. Ultimately the goal of Invaders, the conversions, succeeded as a result of slaughtering their husbands in battles and they (the women) became slaves to whom the Muslim Nobles, Caliphs and

Emperors and ***finally the Muslim soldiers used them for sex on the basis of grades of beauty choice***. Each Muslim indented three to four wives as sanctioned by their Quran these ugly facets of life occurred mostly in the Eastern and Northern part of Sindh of western part of India. This was because of vital tonic prepared by Muslims through *Spices available in plenty in India's southern part of Kerala and annexed Islands. The* ***chemical tonic prepared out of spices was used for deriving aesthetic escalation*** *and in South and West parts it happened on different line that is termed as Sufism.* Around this time on the North-Western part of India especially around Punjab a new ***religion Sikhism started*** and gained popularity.

The Bahamans (13465-1689): The Bahaman Kingdom was founded by Hagan Gangu who led a rebellion against Sultan Muhammad Bin Tughlaq and proclaimed the Independence of the Bahaman Kingdom (1346). He took the title of Bahaman shah and became the first Ruler of the Dynasty. The Kingdom include the whole of the Northern Deccan up to the River Krishna of the Kingdom Vijayanagar Empire with which it had to fight continuous wars for various reasons and *one such reason was **conversion** since South remained untouched with conversions*.

The Most remarkable in the Bahamans Kingdom was Feroz Shah Bahaman (1397-1422) who fought three major Battles with Vijayanagar Empire without any result. He was well acquainted with religion and natural science. He wanted to make Deccan a cultural center of India.

Ferhista, the court poet calls him an orthodox Muslim his only weakness being his fondness for drinking wine in favor of his brother Ahmed Shah who called as Saint (wali) on account of his association with the famous Sufi Gesu Daraz. He invaded Warangal and annexed the most of its territories. The Loss of Warangal changed the balance of Power in South India. The Bahamans Kingdom gradually extended and reached its climax under the Prime Minister of Muhammad Gawan (1466-1481).

One of the most difficult problems which faced the Bahamans was strife among the Nobles who were divided into Deccan (old Comers) and Afaquis and Gharibs (new comers)

Since Gavan was a new comer, it was hard for him to win the confidence of the Deccan's. His broad policy of reconciliation could not stop the partly strife in 1482, Gavan who was over seventy years was executed by Sultan Mohammad Shah of the Deccan. After the death of the Party strife became more intensive and various governors became independent and finally divided in to five parts namely as detailed below. These Kingdom together crusaded against Vijayanagar Empire and defeated in 1565.

Adil Shahi	Of Bijapur
Qutub Shahi	Of Golkonda
Nizam Shahi	Of Ahmednagar
Barid Shahi	Of Bidar
Imad Shahi	Of Birar

Later on Imad Shahi was conquered by Nizam Shahi in 1574; Barid Shahi was annexed by Adil Shahi in 1619. These Kingdoms played a leading role in Deccan politics till their absorption in Mughal Empire during 17th Century. It was Aurangzeb, the Moghul King, who after the death Shivaji marched towards the South and annexed Bijapur (1686) and Golconda in (1689) and brought an end of Bahamans Kingdom. In between these period the *largest domes of World Gol Gumbaz at Bijapur* were the fine example of architecture of this time. Bahamans in many respect were similar to the Delhi Sultanates. The Bahmani Kingdom acted as a culture was developed as a result it had its own specific features which were distinct from North India as the Public Money was used beyond the treasury limits to construct their graves tombs and the standing example is Taj Mahal.

After the death of the party strife became more intensive and various governors became independent and finally divided into five parts namely Adilshahi of Bijapur, Qutub shahi of

Golkonda, Nizamshahi of Ahmed Nagar, and Barid Shahi of Bidar and Imad Shahi of Bidar.

3. The Moghuls (1526-1857):

The Moghul period can be called as *second classical age in North India after Guptha Epire*. In this cultural development the Indian traditions were amalgamated with the Turks-Iranian culture brought to the country Mughals.

Babur (1526-1530): Babur found the Moghul Dynasty, was the King of Kabul. He was invited to India to fight against Lodi (1526) and the result was Babur defeated Lodi at the battle of Panipat. Babur was the first king to bring artillery to India and succeeded because the cavalry that he had bought from Central Asia, which was new to the Indian Army. Before his death Babar made himself the master of the Punjab, Delhi, and Ganga Plains as far as Bihar. He wrote an autobiography "Tuzuk-Babari" containing lovely descriptions of India in Turkish Language.

In his own words on killing Hindus Babur claimed that "For the sake of Islam I became wanderer, I battled infidel and Hindus. I am determined to become a Martyr (Shaheed).Thank god I became a killer of 100,000 Infidels. I became a killer of Non-Muslims!" Which was extracted from Baburnama, the Memories of Babur himself" In Al Hijra 934 (1538). "I attacked Chandlery and by the grace of Allah I captured it within few hours. Begot the Infidels slaughtered and the place which had been called hitherto as *Darul-Harb* (nation of Non-Muslims) for few years I made into a *Darul-Islam* (Muslim Nation)". Gurunanak on Babur's' atrocities said: Source Rag Asa Guru Nanak Dev. witnessed first had the atrocities Babur committed on Hindus and recorded them in his poems. He says "Having attacked Khurassaan *Babur terrified Hindustan*. The Creator himself does not take the blame, but has sent the Moghul as the Messenger of death. There was so much slaughter that the people screamed. Did you feel compassion, Lord? (pg.360) on the condition of Hindu women in Babur's Monster rule: "*Those heads adorned with braided hair, with their parts painted with vermillion- throats were chocked with dust. They lived in palatial mansion but now they cannot even sit near the palaces; ropes put around their necks and their stings of pearls were broken. Their wealth and Youthful beauty which gave them so much pleasure, have now become their enemies. The order was given to the Soldier who dishonored and carried them away with beautiful women. If it pleasing God's will bestow greatness; it pleases his will, He bestows punishment* (Pg.417-18)

On the Nature of Moghul Rule under Babur: First the tree puts down its roots and then spreads out its shade above. *The Kings are tigers and their officials are dogs, they go out and awaken the sleeping people to harass them. The Public servants inflict wounds with their nails. The dog lick up the blood that is spilled.* (Source Rag Malar: Page 1288)

Humayun 1530-1556: He inherited a vast unconsolidated empire and an empty treasury. He had to deal with the growing power of Afghan Sher Shah, from the East who had Bengal and Berar under him. Sher Shah defeated in Kannauj in1540 and Humayun passed to next twelve years in exile that is in 1555, after the death of Sher Shah. Humayun regained the throne from his successor.

Akbar (1556-1605): Humayuns' son Akbar succeeded in 1556. Akbar was an able but ruthless and daring could consolidated the Mughal Empire. He was an idealist, dreamer and yet a man of action and leader of Men who roused the passionate loyal of his followers. He was only thirteen when he came to the throne. His first conflict with Hemu, a general of Adil Shah, under whom the Afghan resistance had regrouped king Hemu, who was the ***only one Hindu who ever ruled the Delhi Throne in Indian History***, at the second battle of Panipat. Hemu was defeated in 1556 and Akbar reoccupied Delhi and Agra.

Akbar annexed Malwa and brought a major part of Rajasthan under his control. ***He build Bulund Darwaja at Fatehpur Sikri*** after his successful campaign and dominating

Gujarat. Most of the Rajasthan were forced to recognize his suzerainty except Mewar, which continued to resist under the great hero Rana Pratap and his lieutenant Amar Singh. After his success in Military activities and administration Akbar's insatiable quest and his personnel need led him *to build the Ibadat Khana –Hall of Prayer (1575).* It was only to the Sunnis but later in 1578 it was opened the people of all religions in an effort to win over those who refused to convert. However, in 1582 he discontinued the debate in the Ibadath Khana. Later in academic, spiritual and metaphysical aspects of it crystalized into Touhi—Ilahi (Divine Monotheism). Akbar did not created new a religion but suggested a new religious path based on the common truths of all religions, which continued to place in supreme position. The word Din (faith) of Din-iIlahi was applied after eighty years.

Akbar claimed to believe that a ruler was the guardian of his subjects and had to look after their welfare irrespective of their creed. A sort of secularism was inaugurated during his period. He claimed a policy of Sulh-i-Kul (peace to all). Because of his attempt to convince the native population he was a generous and tolerant tyrant, he has come to be called by the gullible as one of the great rulers in Indian history*, a lie still believed* by many even today. **Salim (Jahangir) 1605-1627**): Akbar's son Salim succeed his as Jahangir after his death. He strengthened his control over Bengal and his four successive campaign forced Amar Singh of Mewar to accept his suzerainty. Mogul empire became more vulnerable to attack from central and western Asia. Towards the end of his reign he had to deal with the rebellion of his son Shah Jahan.

Shahjehan (1605-1627). On his success to the throne, the first thing he had to face was revolts of Bundelkhand and the Deccan. Marathas also emerged as Major threat to an authority of the Moghuls. He had an active interest taken by Noor Jehan, his queen in matters of the state and also ruled the empire when he was ill. His failing health started a war of succession among his four sons in 1657. He seized and remodeled a great *Shiva*

Temple, the Tejo Mahila and turned it into a grave yard for one of his dead wives and renamed it Tajmahal.

Aurangajeb (1658-1707): Aurangajeb was the third son treacherously emerged victorious by killing his brothers and imprisoned his father in Agra Fort till his death. He ruled for almost 50 years. During his long reign Moghul Empire reached its territorial climax. At its height it stretched from Kashmir in north to Jinji in South and from Hindu Kush in the west to Chittagong in the East. He was an orthodox in his outlook and kept himself with narrow confines of the Islamic Law. He described Akbar supposedly secular principle and vigorously enforced the Jazia Tax on non-Muslims as many Indian Hindus refused to convert in to Islam. *He destroyed many temples and started to raise Mosques in the place of Temples*. This did not make Muslims more loyal to the Islamic state, although, the vast native Hindu majority became even more alienated. Most of his time was spent in trying to put down the revolt in different parts of his empire, while the Empire was rent by strife and revolt, the new Maratha power was growing and consolidation of itself in Western India.

He considered himself "the Scourge of kafirs (non-believers) and closed *Hindu Schools and Libraries*. In his life time he destroyed more than 10,000 Hindu, Buddhist and Jains Temples and often erected mosques in their stead 3 places in 1669 in Agra. He had hacked off the limbs of recalcitrant Hindu King Gokhle in 1672, several thousand revolting Hindus were *slaughtered* in Mewar.

From Maasi Alamgir: he issued general order to destroy all centers of Hindu learning including Varanasi and destroyed temple Mathura and renamed as Islamabad.

In Khadela (Rajasthan, Udaipur Pandhpur of Maharashtra, Aurangzeb slaughtered 10000 Hindus. He also tortured to death the disciples of Guru Tej Bahadur before his death and also killed him. Guru Tej Bahadur –the Pride of Hindustan was martyred for he spoke for the persecuted Hindus, Sikh Children and Made *the Sikh women to eat the flesh of their*

killed children. He announced in public that if anybody gets any Muslim bringing the head of dead Sikh was to be awarded with wealth.

Shivaji the Maratha Hero stopped Aurangzeb's mission of expanding towards South. However, after Shivaji accomplished his mission of Southward expansion apart from him no one else except the British held India under single Rule.

Aurangzeb the last Moghul tried to put the clock back and in his attempt broke up the empire. After his death Mughal empire collapsed with internal conflict among successors and was reduced to the area around Delhi. The provinces declare independence and Marathas under the leadership of Peshawar gradually extended their hold in North India. Foreign invasion of Nadir Shah Abdani in (1729) and Ahmed Shah Abdani in (1747-61) (**Ahmedis also are Kefirs in the outlook of Sunni Muslims**) **further weakened the Empire.** The last Moghul emperor Bahadur Shah Zafar was imprisoned by the British after 1857 Mutiny.

Jahangir (1605-1628) though in the beginning of his rule he followed the humanistic rule of his father Akbar. But later on the plea of Islamic Court Clerics he followed with the steps taken by his great grandfather (Babur). **He tortured Guru Arjun DevJi guru and imprisoned at Lahore fort. He was chained to a post in open place exposed to the Sun from morning to evening in hottest Summer in the Months of May and June Below his feet a heap of sand was put which burnt like a furnace boiling water was poured on his naked body at intervals. His body was covered with blisters all over. In this agony Guru used to utter** "Tera jiya meetha Lage, naam padrath Nanak mane (What every you ordain appears sweet to you, I supplicate for the fight of name and later Guru was executed.

4. Portuguese (1510):

India's connection with the West has predominantly related to **Spice trade**. Among the modern Europeans, the Portuguese were the first to establish themselves in India and the last of the Europeans to leave. They arrived as early as 1498 via the ocean route discovered by Vasco-da-Gama. He was the first discover of sea route via Cape of Good Hope to India, when Constantinople came under the Arab Power. Portuguese left behind Raman Catholic Christianity with its Baroque Churches, its musical liturgy and its great Monastic order committed to educate. *Europe had much to steal from India such as spices, textiles and other oriental products*.

The best classical accounts are in fact the commercial ones. When direct contact was lost with the fall of Rome and the rise of Muslims, the trade was carried on through middleman. In the late middle ages it increased with increasing prosperity through Europe, it should be remembered that the spice trade was not solely a luxury trade at that time. *Spice were needed to preserve meat*, through winter (cattle had to be slaughtered in the late autumn through lack of winter fodder) and to combat the taste of the decay. Wine in the absence of ancient or modern the threat of Mongol and Turkish invasion which interfered with the land routes and threatened to engulf the sea route Egypt and there was the threat of Monopoly shared between the Venetians and Egyptians.

In 1510 Alfonse de Albuquerque capture the Island of Goa as the west coast of India from the Sultan of Bijapur and made it the capital of the Portuguese Eastern Empire Alfonso de Albuquerque capture the Island of Goa, as the west coast of India from the Sultan of Bijapur and made it the capital of the Portuguese Eastern Empire. Its strong points besides Goa were Socotra off the Red Sea (he could not take Aden), Ormuz in the Persian, Din in Gujarat, Malacca, enter pot for the far east and the *spice trade in the East Indies* and Macao in China. The function of Goa was to supervise Malabar, to control the pilgrim traffic to Mecca as well as general trade to Egypt, Iraq and Persia, and of Malacca to control the *East Indian Spices at their source*.

However the Portuguese irked some of the Moghul and preceding Rulers because of the toll they took of the trade from the port of Surat and pilgrim traffic. In seizing and retaining their strong points they acquired a reputation for cruelty and perfidy because their practice on both these points was below the current Indian standard. They deeply ***impregnated with the idea that no faith need be kept with an infidel***. This was the *standard impression the Europeans and Arabs had on the Hindus*. It was from this period the word Feringi (literary meaning is Frank) acquired the opprobrium of which echoes may still be heard today. ***That was the impression Europeans and Arabs had Indian Hindu and Europeans and Arabs are frank in dealing is the impression they earned from Hindus***). However the Mughal emperor Jahangir admired their pictures and then copied. Emperor Akbar listened with interest to Jesuit Father's discourses. The New Testament was Christianity and Islam became gradually more intense, both are the offshoots of Abrahamic Religion, and that is the reason they join each other on other religions particularly Hindus who are Infidel to whom their God, Allah Hate as per their Holy Scriptures Bible and Quran. In 1519 Ferdinand Magellan, a Portuguese Navigator commanded the first expedition to sail around the world, In the Collins Encyclopedia it is written that Magellan set seal to check the Power of Muslim navy and fleet that was dominant . In 1560 the Portuguese being intolerant in Religion, introduced the inquisition with all its horrors. This was regarded as the sub-standard from the Indian stand point, advertising this trait in their rough handling of Syrian Christians of Malabar to secure their submission to Catholic faith.

Socially the policy of Albuquerque in encouraging mixed marriage had important results. His object was to rear a population possessing Portuguese blood imbued with Portuguese catholic culture who would be committed by race and taste to Portuguese settlements and so form a permanent self-perpetuated garrison. The result was race ***long known as Luso-Indians and now on Goanese or Goans***. They are mainly Indian in blood, catholic in religion and partially Western outlook. In recent times they have spread all over India as traders and professionals, a less successful version of Parsis (of all the Asian in Britain a majority of whom are Muslim, the Asian MP had to be Roman Catholic of Goanese descent, Keith Vaz) Some Portuguese words have even crept in to Urdu language such as name of items for furniture (mayze for desk, almirah for cupboard/wardrobe) Also *Vindaloo* (curry) is part for Portuguese for meat and aloo is the Urdu word for potato- thus we have meat and potato curry)

The Portuguese were soon followed by European rivals like the French, Dutch, East India company winning South East Asia and Indonesia (known to Europeans as the East Indies) and the British "East India company having to settle for second best that is India.

5. Dutch East Company 1602-1795:

By Charter of Holland, the Dutch India Company was established in 1602. As the Dutch company was interested very much interested in Spice Trade they had their focus on the Far East and made India their trading depot. In 16106, they established their factories at Petapalli and Masulipatnam. Realizing that Indian textiles have a large market they established factories at Pulicat in 1610, Combay in 1620, Surat and Agra in 1621, Haripur in 1633, Patna in 1638, Decca in 1650, Udaigiri in 1651, Sinsura in 1653, Qasim Bazar in Bangalore, Balasure and Nagapatnam in 1659, Dutch withdrew from Golkonda by 1684. They also opened factories in Bengal, Khankal in 1669 and at Malda in 1676 and but both were closed soon.

The rising Dutch power was looked as *threat* by the British and a truce was concluded between them in 1619 but it was not lasting. By 1795 the British expelled Dutch from India totally.

6. French East India Company:

French were the last of the Europeans to enter to Eastern India Trade before British. The French East India Company was established in 1664. In 1668 the first French Factory was established in Surat. The French established their second factory Masulipatnam in 1669. The French obtained Pondierry in 1673 and they built Chandrangore in 1690-92. There was rivalry between the British and the Dutch for Major share in the Eastern trade.

Further the hostile relations between these powers in Europe also led to war in India. There was hostility between the French and Dutch in 1690 and again in 1721. The French and British companies clashed India between 1742 and 1760. The French hopes of establishing their political powers came to an end in 18th century. In the beginning the French had their headquarters at Surat but later they shifted to Pondicherry. The supreme body of French was known as "Superior Council of the Indies". It was headed by Director General and he was p laced in charge of the French affairs in India. The Superior Counsel constituted of a Governor and five members.

The mutual jealousies and quarrels between the French Officials and commanders in India, which ultimately after 1789, the French East India trade thrown open to Individuals. In a way the French who initiated the strategy of interfering in internal affair so f Indian states to obtain political mileage and showed the way to the British. While French failed in their strategy, it is the British who were successful. Besides the Portuguese the Dutch the British and the French, The Danes entered in as traders in 1616 and obtained Trancquabar part from the Nayak of Tanjaore in 1620 and built a fort there. Likewise the Swedish East India did business for a short while and the activities of Flanders Merchants were also limited to India alone for a short while. The discovery of the new sea route via Cape of Good Hope, throw the Eastern traded open to all European nations. Through they started factories at Masulipatnam post Novo and Serampur their success in trading business was short lived as the sources were scanty. They sold the factories to the British and left India in 1845.

The European Trade and colonization of India and fighting among the European Companies to decide who to control the India, recalled a *simile* from Japanese class in High school as follows"

I think it has relevance to the current situation:

"Title of the story "A monkey and four cats:

Once upon a time two cats found a piece of Cheese and cut it into two pieces. But one piece was slightly bigger than the other. But the two cats wanted the bigger piece. Then they went to a monkey and asked to sort out the matter.

The Monkey said "Don't worry. I will make both the pieces equal" Then it took a bite from the bigger piece. But this made the other piece larger. So it took a bite from the other piece. This continued till the pieces became very small. Seeing this the cats pleaded "Sir we are satisfied. Let us have the pieces now." The Shrewd monkey replied "This is my fee for sorting out the problem" saying this it gobbled up the remaining cheese." The End. Likewise cats represents Portuguese and France and shrewd monkey is British and made the entire India as its colony. How the India became its colony following sections will elucidate.

7. Maratha King Chatrapathi Shivaji

The Maratha Rebel Shivaji was born in 1727 the Shivery in Maharashtra in Western India. The Maratha's were the first who crossed Malik Kafur's Path and he invaded Deccan 1314. They were led by Yadava Dynasty. The Maratha's before Shivaji were mercenaries and revenue collectors for the Muslim Rulers in keeping with the feudal tradition, the Maratha Sardar's (generals) before Shivaji kept shifting their loyalties from one Muslim to another.

Shivaji's mother JiJiabai was direct descendent of erstwhile Yadava royal family of Devagiri. She seems to have nursed deep within her mind the idea of recovering Independence from Muslim rule when Shivaji was 17th de decided to transform what were till the games to reality. With the blessing of his mother JiJiabai Shivaji founded the Hindu Kingdom in the Deccan against the odds fighting's against the tyranny of Moghul Ruler Aurangzeb. He inspired and united the common man to fight against the tyranny of Mughal ruler Aurangzeb by making sense of pride and Nationality in them. At the age 16, he took to establish a sovereign Hindu State. He clearly outstands all the Rulers and generals of India by the exemplary life he lived and is thus respected by the entire cross section of Indians. Shivaji is to India what Napoleon was to Europe.

He raised a strong army and Navy, constructed and repairs forts, used guerilla warfare tactics, developed a strong intelligence network, gave equal treatment to the People from all religions and castes based on Merit functioned like a seasoned statesman and General. He appointed ministers with specific functions such as internal security, foreign affairs finance law and Justice, religious matters defense etc.

He introduced systems in revenue collection and warned the Officials against harassment of subjects. He thought ahead of times and was a true visionary. In his private life, his moral virtues were exceptionally high. His thought and deeds were inspired by the teaching of his mother JiJiabai, teacher Dadaji Konddev great saints like Dayaneswar and Tukaram and the valiancy and ideals of Lord Krishna. The Kingdom established by Chatrapathi Shivaji known as 'Haindavi Swaraj (Sovereign Hindu State) spread beyond attack in North West India (now in Pakistan) and beyond Cuttack in East India in course of Time, to become the strongest Power in India. The Peshavas (Pune) Shinde Gwalior (Baroda) and Holkar (Indore) contributed to the growth. The history of India is incomplete without the history of Maratha, Shivaji has been source of Inspiration and pride and will continue to inspire generations in future.

On invitation by Aurangzeb Shivaji presented himself at Moghul Court, Aurangzeb deliberately insulted him by making stand behind the lessor Noble to whom Shivaji had once defeated in battle. This was a calculated humiliation that Aurangzeb had arranged for Shivaji. As a result of this he left the court. This gave Aurangzeb an excuse to declare Shivaji of having committed the offence of insulting the Moghul court. Then Aurangzeb detained him in Mirza Rajasing's house where Shivaji stayed. However, Shivaji was very sharp to know that he was trapped and will be killed and hence he escaped the detention. As long as Shivaji lived there was peace for 25 years, no attempts of invasion was taken up by Moghul Emperor, but because of the internal troubles it is reported that he was poisoned to death in April 1680

8.British East India Company:

The East India Company charted by the British Crown and ultimately responsible to the parliament launched British was established under Royal Charter of Queen Elizabeth I for 15 years **Spice Trading** on 31st December 1600 AD with capital of 70,000 pounds.

By the Middle of the 18th century the company succeeded in establishing power in Bengal, Bihar Orissa and the East Coast. After the battle of Plassy in 1757 they secured permission from Moghuls to collect land revenue from these provinces in return for an annual tribute and maintaining of order and peace.

They collected the land revenues through local Nawab and took control of his army. This gave them power without responsibility. The Company took control of Mysore trade by defeating Tipu Sultan in 1792 and Marathas were finally defeated in 1817 AD and 1819 AD. Further the company and its rule by defeating Nepal in 1814-61, Sindh in 1843, Punjab in 1848-49 and Burma in 1886. The cruel Management of the company ultimately led to the Mutiny of 1857 after which its rule over India ended and the British crown officially took over the admission in 1856.

9. Sepoy Mutiny of 1857:

After nearly century of British rule the many changes that Britain had brought about the administration and the way of life created considerable discontent that were many risings in various parts of the Country from 1816 to 1857. This cumulated in the revolt of 1857 which took the very foundation of company's rule in India. The spirit rule was growing especially amongst feudal chiefs and their followers. Even amongst the masses discontent and in an intense and British feeling was wide spread in March 1857. The Indian Army at Barrackpore mutinied and his spread rapidly lit wild fire and assumed the character of popular rebellion and was a war Independence.

By the material was upheaval was ready and required only a spark to get it fire. The episode of greased cartridges provided this spark and the revolt was started by Mangal Pande. The greased cateridges which were to be chewed before firing contained facts of cow and pig. The cow was holy for the Hindus whereas pig was the most unholy for Muslims. Immediately the revolt engulfed North and Central India. On May 10 1857 Sepoy stationed at Meerut mutinied and marched to Delhi and proclaimed Bahadur Shah Zafar the last Moghul Emperor as the last Moghul Emperor of India.

10. The British Rule over India:

The Revolt of 1857 jolted the British administration in India and forced its reorganization. By the Act of Governing Power was transferred from the East India Company to the British Crown. This power was to be exercised by the Secretary of the State of India (Member of the British Cabinet and responsible to Parliament aided by an Indian council which head only advisory powers. For administrative purpose India was divided into three presidencies namely Bengal Madras and Bombay presidency. The interests of the British thus became paramount in the Government of India.

Soon after Dyer's arrival on the afternoon of April 13 1919, some 10,000 or more unnamed folk both Men and women gathered in Amritsar's at Jallianwala Baag (Baag-Garden) to conduct protest meeting, despite a ban on Public assemblies. It was Sunday and many neighboring villages' peasants came to Amritsar to celebrate the Hindu Baaisakhi Spring Festival. Dyer positioned his men at the Sole narrow passage way of the Garden (Baag). *Giving no word of warning he ordered 50 soldiers to fire into the gathering and for 10 to 15 minutes, 1650 rounds of ammunition were unloaded into screaming of terrified crowds. According to official estimates nearly 4000 civilians were killed, 1200 left wounded with no medical attention.* Dyer argued that his action was necessary to produce a "Moral widespread effect and the governor of Punjab province also supported the Massacre and on April 15 the placed the entire province under martial Law.

The Policies and interests of the British empire in other parts of the world and in costly wars. The queen's proclamation of 1858 promised not to extend British territories in India by annexing princely states and they were subordinated to the British government by the act of 1876, queen Victoria assumed the title of Empress if India. This implied that the Britain would protect the Indian states from internal as well as external danger and get the unlimited powers to intervene in the internal affairs of the State.

Thus after 1857 India was divided into two parts British India, directly governed by the British government and the Indian states ruled by Indian princes. Brightness gradually stopped their support to the reforms which resulted in the preservation of social evils. After 1857 Mutiny they followed the Divide and Rule Policy in aim to create a rift between the Indians (Hindus) and Muslims.

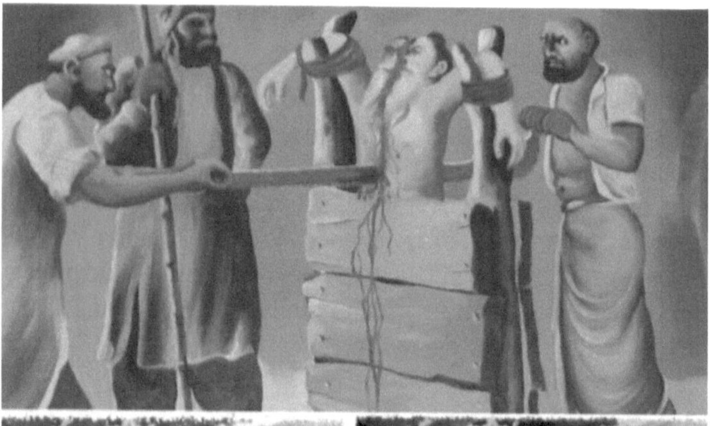

CHAPTER 6

CAUSES OF SUCCESS OF TURK INVADERS AND PERSECUTION OF HINDUS

Earlier section gave a vivid picture of invasions of various civilizations on Hindu civilization. But the question arises why the Muslims and European invasions were proved success. Why did not we have strong ruling dynasties like Mouryans and Guptha dynasties in the earlier late medieval period? Are we inefficient warriors? Is there any inadequacy of Nationalism in the Kings and Nobles of our Indian Sovereignty in resisting the invasions? Let us sort out the reasons to reply these questions just raised.

(I) Major Cause that helped invaders to be successful: The Mourya Empire (322-1`85 BCE) the first Unity India into one State and was the largest on the Indian Sub-continent. At its greatest the Mouryans Empire stretched the North up to the Natural boundaries of Himalayas and East into what now Assam. To the West it reached was established by Chandragupta Mourya assisted by Chanakya (Koutilya) in Magadha (in Modern times Bihar when he over threw the Nanda Dynasty.

Chandragupta son of Bindusara succeeded to throne around 297 BCE. By the time he died in 272 BCE a large part of the subcontinent was under Mouryans suzerainty. However the region of Kalinga (Modern Odisha) renamed outside Mouryans control perhaps interfering with Spice trade with South. Bindusara was succeeded by Asoka whose reign lasted for around 37years until his death in about 232 BCE. His campaign against Kalinga in about 260BCE though successful lead to immense loss of life and Misery. This filled Asoka with *remorse and led him to shun violence* and subsequently to embrace Buddhism. This Empire began to decline after his death and the last Mouryans ruler Brihadatta was assassinated by Pushyamitra Suhunga to establish Sunga Empire.

(ii) Second major cause for the success of Invaders was Bhakti Movement: Early medieval India began after the end of Guptha Empire in 6th Century. This period also covers the late classical Age of Hinduism which began after the end of Guptha Empire and the collapse of Empire of Harsha in 7th Century CE the beginning of Imperial Kanouj leading to tripartite struggle and ended in the 13th century with the rise of Delhi Sultanate in North India and the end of late Cholas with the death of Rajendra Chola III in 1279 in southern India however all aspect of classical period continued until the fall of Vijayanagar Empire in South around 17th Century .

In 7th century Kumara Bhatta formulated his school of Mimamsa philosophy and fended the position on Vedic rituals against Buddhist attack. In 8thCentury Adi Sankaracharya travelled across subcontinent to propagate and spread of doctrine of Advaita Vedanta, which consolidated and is credited with unifying main characteristics of current thoughts in Hinduism. He was critic of both Buddhism and Mimamsa School for Hinduism and founded Mathas (Monasteries). In the four corners of the Indian subcontinent he spread and solidified the development of Advaita Vedanta. However, royal proclivities for the cults of Vishnu and Shiva weakened Buddhists position within the socio political context and helped make possible its decline. Meanwhile there was a growth of Muslim population. Later the death of Prithviraj Chouhans caused Raj Puts to prevent to counter attack invasion Muslims. Bhakti movement campaigned by Sankaracharya and rise of Buddhism and Sikhism that preach Non-violence that contributed for the promotion of peace. This theistic approach both by commoners and Nobles harvested lethargic breed to counter the invasions.

Few more causes that made India defeated by Muslim invasions: Every invasion of Muslims had to be destined to face by Rajputs who were protecting India's' sovereignty. It is an irony of fate that Rajput's exemplary warriors in their political arena. Rajput were paragon with rare bravery, chivalry and valor that lost to the Turk Invaders who came from barren destitute and distant deserted lands. There are few more reasons to be assigned to their phenomenon defeat which include:

1. Political causes
2. Military causes
3. Religious causes
4. Social causes and
5. Geographical causes.

1. Political causes

A. There was no powerful central authority in India that could have offered strong resistance to the Invaders, as did the Magadha Empire at the time of Greek Invasion to India at that time was divided into a number of Independent Raj Put States.

B. Disunity among Rajputs Rulers: As stated by Dr. Ishwar Prasad "*State fought against state* for leadership as there was no *paramount power* which could effectively hold them together by any principle of Unity or cohesion" they were taught mutual fights among Raj put States, particularly among the Chauhan's and Rathores, , the Chandelles and Chalukyas and Pratihara, Palas and RashtraKutakas. According to Chandbardai "Ninety out of hundreds of Pruthiviraj's Samantha's (chiefs) fell in this conflicts with Jaiachand on account of his carrying away Samyuktha".

C. *Lack of Political insight*: Even series of Muslims invasions did not produce a single Rajput ruler with Political insight to visualize as to what would happen to all of them, one by one if the foreign in roads were not faced and checked unitedly.

D. *Neglect of Frontiers*: The Rajput rulers failed to evolve any frontier policy could not forget their internal feuds and rise above personal prejudices to save the frontier states being crushed under the foreign soldiers.

E. Feudalism: The army of a Rajput ruler was constituted by collecting the armies of feudal chief than to the ruler. Feudal system led the weakling of the power of the King.

2. Military Causes:

A. Interior war art: In the words of Dr. VA Smith "Hindu Kings though fully equal to their assailants in courage and contempt of death, were ***distinctly inferior*** in the art of war and for that reason lost their independence."

B. Lack of appropriate military strategy: The Rajput army advanced with all the wings together –the right, the center and the left. The Turks used a special strategy with their two units-one advanced guard and other the reserve. The advance guard was meant to test the strength and to find out weakness areas, the reserve was thrown into the battle fray after the Rajputs' had exhausted their resources.

C. Lack of offensive: Rajputs mostly fought defensive battles with foreign invaders and this was not appropriate way of winning a battle.

D. Outdated weapons and war strategy: Rajput did not try to find out the latest techniques and weapons used in foreign lands.

E. Elephant versus horses: The Rajput depended to a considerable extent upon the elephants. The elephants were easily stuck with fear with the swiftness of the horses' movements and the war cries. They ran helter-skelter spreading fear and disorder their own camp. The strength of Turks lay in their efficient cavalry.

F. *Lack of military leadership* is quite different from bravery and chivalry. The Rajput rulers and their commanders did not have the requisite capacity to infuse zeal in their armies. On the other hands the Turk, invaders could easily arouse the battle cry "to do or die".

G. Over dependence on the ruler: Usually the soldiers of the Rajput rulers had the impression that after the death or disappearance of the Raja, they could not face the enemy. The disappearance of the Raja/King even for a short while created panic in the army. The disappearance of Amanda Pal for a while when his Elephant was hit by an arrow caused panic and his army lost heart and consequently battle against Mahmud Ghazni **Lane-Poole** has described the fate of the war as **"Amanda Pal's elephant took fright**, the rumor ran that the Raja was fleeing from the field vague suspicious and distrust spread about, and a general stampede ensued. Instead of retreating before vivacious army, in an instant Mahmoud found himself pursuing a panic stricken crowd

H. Only Rajput is in the array: Only Rajput had the duty to fight. Other classes were in different. Thus too much dependence on the Rajput was the weakness of the Military organization.

3. Religious Causes:

A. Ghazi Spirit of the Muslim army: A **Ghazi is one who gives his life in defense of Islam.** According to Lane Poole "The very bigotry of the creed (Muslims) was an instrument of Self-preservation." For Muslim soldiers, the fight against the Rajput that is the Hindu was a Jihad (Holy War) - a crusade to protect as well as spread their religion. The soldiers were thoroughly convinced that if they died for their religion they would go to Paradise. If they won, they would get all the pleasure of the World, besides being the protectors of the Religion.

B. No Unitary ideology of the Hindus: Hinduism had no unified ideology to bind them together to the extent the Muslims had.

C. Impact or Buddhism: Buddhist concept of Ahimsa did great harm to the Martial spirit of the Hindus. It made the **Hindus timid and peace loving**. They have only **Bhakti to adorn the gods** and cherish their desires. As such they were more inclined to tie with liberation (Moksha).

4. Social causes:

A. Decaying society: The caste system in Hind India had divided Hindu Society and injected the venom of hatred humiliation and inequality, prejudice and untouchability. On contrary, Islam infused a spirit of brotherhood. It has been observed that the Fellowship of equal brother hood in Islam surpassed in unity and strength in the world. Further the Islamists states that theory of All Human are equal and there is no question of compartmentalized life like, Brahman, Vysya, Kshatriya and Sudra in terms of caste on the Hindu platform. Further there is a universal life brother hood and there is no hypothesis exists to title human being is related to a particular caste or race. However they have two divisions in their religion that is Faithful or Muslim and *Infidel* and hence the it is the duty of each Muslim to wage war against Infidel

*B. Superstition of Hindu*s: In the words of V.C. Vaidya "*superstition acted like a double edged sword* towards the full of Hindu India, while the Muslims believed that victory has bound to come to them, the Hindus believed that they were bound to be conquered by the Muslims in *Kaliyuga*. Such superstition demoralized and discouraged the Hindus."

C. Slave system of the Muslim Rulers: The slaves maintained by the Muslim Rulers were very faithful to their masters. They were promised adequate opportunities to hold their high offices according to their ability. They were always ready to die for their masters.

D. Administrative Factors: The Rajput did not set up an efficient spy system to be adequately acquainted themselves with the overall position of their adversaries. It is also very unfortunate that some time Rajput officials proved treacherous as they let out some of the military secrets to the enemy.

5. Geographical causes:

Some historians have suggested that the hot climate of India sapped the strength and vigor of the Indiana Soldiers. The

Muslim soldiers came from cold regions and were habitually hard and study. They were not bothered by the Indian heat as they were used to face climatic harshness. *"Heat or Cold" the mission they carried with was to see the end of Infidels, as ordered by their Prophet and Allah of their religion and this factor was the ultimate goal to conquer the Indian idolaters at any cost and that was the only matter that mattered them and this zeal made them to achieve victory*. More so the Muslim had an excellent recruiting grounds in the land beyond the chilling Afghan Hills from which they could constantly bring new recruits to fight against the Hindus.

B. *Economic Factors*: Large number of soldiers of the Turk invaders were attracted by the wealth of India. They, therefore, fought with full zeal. As already stated religious fanaticism was also the encouraged them. Thus the two factors combined together to infuse vigor in them. The wealth of the temples, however, not maintained and protected properly. It, therefore became easy for invaders to plunder these places and demoralized the Indian Rajput.

Before concluding, let us pay our attention to what our great Historians said in this context. According to Dr. Ishwari Prasad "There was no dearth of military talent or fighting skill in the country, for Rajput's were the finest soldiers scarcely inferior in the quality of courage, valor and endurance to men of any other country. But they *lacked Unity and organization*. Pride and Prejudice alike forbade obedience to a common leader and in crucial movements when concentrated action was essential for a victory. They used to renew their individual plans and thus neutralized the advantages they possessed over the enemies" Secondly, according to Professor KA Nizami "The real cause of the defeat of the Indians lay in their social system and invidious caste distinction which rendered the whole military organization *rickety and weak.*" Thirdly, R.C. Dutta has emphasized that the Hindus had reached the last stage of their political, religious and social decline at that time and therefore became an easy prey to the invading Turks. Fourthly according Dr. A.L. Srivastava "the absence of the Hindus and the superiority of the Turks in Military organization, skill and resources were responsible for the success of the Turks and "Finally according to ABM Habibullah writes "Raj Put's recklessness has an element of romance in it but is of little practical wisdom.

SECTION (B)
EFFCTS/RESULTS OF INVASION OF HINDU INDIA.

The Islamic conquest of India is probably the bloodiest in the story in the History of India. India's early civilization people have experienced religious persecution in the form of forced conversion, documented massacres, demolition and desecration of Temples, as well as destruction of Universities and Schools in Modern Times. Hindu in Muslim majority regions of Kashmir, Pakistan, Bangladesh, Afghanistan and countries have suffered persecution.

Medieval persecution by Muslim rulers: As we have assessed the causes in earlier section, Muslim conquests of the Indian sub-continent began during the 8th centuries AD. According to 1900 translation of Persian text Chachanamah by Mirza Kalich Baig OF Damascus, Hajjaj responded to plea by men and women attached and imprisoned by a tribe of the coast of Debal (Karachi) who had gone there to purchase some Indian female slaves and rich goods Hajjaj Mobilized an expedition of 6,000 cavalry under Muhammad- bin- Qasim in 712. Records from the campaign recorded in the chachnama record temples demolitions and mass execution resisting Sindh forces and the enslavement of the dependents. The raids attacked the Kingdoms ruled by Hindu and Buddhist Kings wealth plundered, tribute (khara) settled and hostages taken. Numerous Hind Jats were capture as prisoners of war by the Muslim army and moved to Iraq elsewhere *as slaves*.

Parts of India have historically be subjected to Islamic rule from the period of Mohammad bin-Qasim, to the Sultanate and Mogul Empire, as well as smaller kingdoms like Bahamani

Sultanate and Tipu sultan's Kingdom of Mysore. After the conquest of Sindh, Qasim chose the Hanafi School of Islamic law which then under Muslim rule, Polytheist such as Hindus, Buddhists and Jains are to be regarded as Dhimmis (an Arab Term for paid slave) as well as 'People of the Book and are required to pay Jizya for religious freedom.

The decision proved crucial in the Muslim rulers ruled in India for the next 800 years. Historians K.S.Lal in his book 'Theory and practice of Muslim state in India claims that between the year 1000 AD and 1500AD the growth of Muslim Population in medieval India mean while he claimed that the Indian sub-continent decreased Hindu population from 200 to 120million by establishment of Moghul "Empire because of Killings, deportation, dissemination, wars and famines. He stated that his estimates were tentative and not exhaustive.

These population estimates however have been questioned by Simon Dig by and Irfan Habib. Will Durant calls the Muslim conquests of India probably the bloodiest story in History? During this period Buddhism declined rapidly while Hinduism faced military led and sultanates sponsored religious violence. Even those Hindus who converted to Islam were not immune from Persecution, which was illustrated by the Muslim caste system around 20) in India as established by Zia Uddin al-Baroni in the Fatwa-e-Jahandari.

The destruction of Temples and educational institutions killing of learned monks and scattering of students led to a wide spread decline in *Hindu Education with fall of Hindu kings science, research and philosophy faced setbacks due to lack of funding, royal support and open environment.* Despite unfavorable treatment under the Muslim rule, Brahmanical education, continued and was patronized by rulers like Akbar and others. Bukkaraya I, one of the founders of Vijayanagar Empire, had taken steps to rehabilitation of Hindu religious and a cultural institution which suffered a serious setback under Muslim rule.

These are the routine contention and orthodox views revealed about the Muslim Invasion. If you peep further in the past of the Invasion with detailed perspective, following facts and figures about Muslims during their invasions are revealed which include:

Muslim Historian (Mohammad Qasim Hind Shah, (born in 1560 and died in 1620) the Turkish Ferhista gives vivid picture of the genocide, torture, enslavement that and Gulshan Ibrahim was the first to give an Idea to the *Medieval blood bath* that was India faced during Muslim, when he declared that *400 million Hindus got slaughtered, enslaved and castrated. India's population is said to have been around 600 million at the time of Muslim invasion* (711 AD). By 1500's Hindu population was 200 Million. By the time the British arrived to the shores of India and after centuries of Islamic ruling India, the Hindu population was not behaving like their normal self (like Hindus) but they were behaving like Muslims.

There are much witness reports from the British archives of horrendous Hindu incident that were shocking in cruelty to the British-and they therefore some time referred to the people as '*savages*'. It seems they were shocked seeing the behavior of Hindus in that way, since the impression they have heard about Hindus was different. *Politeness* was the symbol of their behavior. Yes, anyone who is contaminated by the association with Islamic 'culture' truly gets tainted and savaged. That is exactly why it is so detrimental and dangerous.

Today, like others with a soul massacred by Islam India is not truly Hindu nation. India is a shadow of Islam, a Hindufied version of Islam, where every human activity has been emulated and adopted into a culture previously alien to such brutality. And in association with a foreign *Mohammadans pest*, there, these Islamic habits have become adopted and accepted as '*normal' as normal part of Indian culture. But if we look at preIslamic Indian culture it was in general a benevolent culture of Knowledgeable and learning* more so than it is today, as we heard from above sections.

*From the time of the Umayyad Dynasty (711 AD to the Moghul Bahadur Shah Jafar 1858) so widely praised as great leaders by Indian who one hitherto pro-British historians, entire cities were burnt down and population massacred with hundred if thousands killed in every campaign and similar numbers deported as slaves. Every new invader made (often literally) his **hills of Hindu skulls**. Thus the conquest of Afghanistan in the year 1000 was followed by the annihilation of the Hindu population; the region is still called Hindu Kush that the Hindu slaughter or Pyre.*

The genocide suffered by Hindu Sikh and Buddhists of India at the hands of Arab Turks, Moghuls and Afghans occupying forces for a period of 800 years, is it formally unrecognized by the world. The similar generous recent past was that of the Jewish people at the hand of Nazis

The a holocaust of the Hindus in India was even greater proportion, the only difference was that it is continued for 800years till the brutal regimes were effectively overpowered in a life and death struggle by the Sikhs in the Punjab and the Hindus armies in other parts of Indian in the 1700s.

We have elaborate literary evidence of the world's biggest holocaust from existing historical contemporary eye witness accounts. *The historians and biographers of the invaders armies and subsequent rulers of India have left detailed records of atrocities* they committed in their day to day encounters with Indian Hindus.

These contemporary records boasted about and glorified the crimes were committed and the genocide of tens and millions of Hindus, mass rape of Hindu women and the destruction of thousands of ancient Hindu/Buddhist Temples and Stupas, and libraries have been documented and provide solid proof of the world's biggest holocaust.

Dr. Kennard Elst in his article states "was there an Islamic Genocide of Hindus states" Medieval persecution by Muslim rulers began during the 8th century AD. According 1900 translation of Persian Text called "*Chachanamah*" by **Mirza Kalich Baig of Damascus,** Hajjaj responded to the plea by men and woman attacked and imprisoned a tribe off the coast of Debal (Karachi) who had gone there to purchase some Indian female slaves and rich goods. Hajjaj mobilized an expedition of 6000 cavalry under Mohammad Bin- Qasim in 712. Records form the campaign recorded in the Chachnama record temple demolitions and Mass executions of resisting Sindh forces and enslavement of the dependents. The raids attacked the kingdoms ruled by Hindus. Kings wealth plundered, tribute (Khara) settled and hostages taken. Numerous Hindu Jats were capture as prisoners of war by the Muslim army and moved to Iraq Elsewhere as slaves.

Parts of India have historically been subject to Islamic from the period of Mohammad bin Qasim, to the Sultanate and Moghul Empire, as well as smaller kingdoms like Bahamani Sultanate and Tipu Sultan's kingdom of Mysore. After the conquest of Sindh, Qasim chose the *Hanafi school of Islamic* Law which that when under Muslim Rule, Polytheists such as Hindus, Buddhists and Jains are to be regarded as Dhimmis (From Arab term means slavery) as well as People of the Book and are required to pay Jizya for religious freedom. The decision proved crucial in to the way which Muslim rulers ruled India for the next 800 years.

Dr. Koenaraad Elst further states that "the first glance at important testimonies by Muslim Chroniclers suggest that over 13 centuries and a territory as vast as the sub-continent, Muslim Holy warriors easily Killed more Hinds more than millions of caused to Holocaust. Ferhista list several occasions when Bahmani sultans in central India killed a hundred thousand of Hindus, "which they set a minimum goal whenever they felt like punishing the Hindu and they were only a third rank provincial dynasty"

The biggest slaughters took place during the raids Mahmoud Ghaznavi (CE1000) during the actually conquest north India by Mohammad Ghuri and his lieutenant (1192CE) and under the Delhi Sultanate (1206-1526). He also writes in his book "Negation in India "the Muslim conquests down to 16th century were for the Hindus a pure struggle of Life and death. Entire cities were burnt down and populations massacred with hundreds of thousands killed every campaign and similar numbers deported as slaves.

Will Durant again argued in his book "The Story of Civilization: Our Oriental Heritage (p.455)

"The Mohammadans conquest of India probably the bloodiest story in the History. The Islamic Historians and Scholars have recorded with great glee and pride that the slaughter of Hindus forced conversions abduction of Hindu women and children to slave markets and the destruction of temples carried out by the warriors of Islam during 800AD to 1700AD. Millions were either converted by sword or massacred during this period."

Francois Gautier in his Book "Rewriting Indian History (1996) wrote : *"The Massacres persecuted by Muslims in India are unparalleled in history bigger than the Holocaust of the Jews by the Nazis or the massacre of the Armenians by the Turks, more extensive even than the slaughter of the South American native populations by invading Spanish and Portuguese."*

Alain Danieou in his book de-I'nde writes:

*"From the time Muslims arriving around 632 AD the history of India becomes a long monotonous series of Murders, Massacres, spoliation, rape, and destruction of heritage Temples. It is a usual in the name of "**holy War**" of their faith, of their sole God that the barbarians have destroyed civilizations wiped out entire races."*

Irfan Husain in his article "***Demons from the past***" observes that: *"While historical events should be judged in the context of the times it cannot be desired that even in that bloody period of History, no mercy was shown to the Hindus. It is un-fortunate enough to be in the path of either the Arab conquerors of Sindh* and South Punjab of the Central Asian who swept in from Afghanistan.

The Muslim Heroes who figure larger than life in our history books committed some dreadful crime. Mohammad Ghazni, Qutubuddin Aibak, Balban, Mohammad Qasim and Sultan Mohammad Tughlaq, all have blood stained hands that the passage of years has not cleansed seen through Hindu eye, the Muslim invasion of their homeland was unmitigated disaster.

The Temples were razed, their Idols smashed, the women raped, men killed or enslaved. When Mahmoud of Ghazni entered Somanatha on one of his annual raids he slaughtered all 50,000 inhabitants. Aibak killed and enslaved hundreds and thousands. **The list of horrors is long and painful**. These conquerors justified their deeds by claiming **it was their religious duty to smite non-believers**. Cloaking themselves in the banner of Islam they claimed they were fighting for their faith when in reality they were indulging in straight forward slaughter and pillage."

A sample of contemporary eye witness, by the Secretary documents through his Book *"Tariq-i-Yamani of the invaders, during the Indian Conquests. "The Afghan Ruler Mahmoud Ghazni invaded India no less than 17times during 1001-1026 AD several episodes of his bloody military campaigns. The blood of the infidels flowed so copiously at the Indian city Thanesar that the stream was **discolored not withstanding its purity** and the people were unable to it ...the infidels deserted the fort and tried to cross the foaming the River Sind... but many of them were slain, taken or drowned nearly fifty thousand men were killed."*

The Persian Historian Wassaf writes in his book "Taziyat-ul-Amsar-wa Tajriyar ul asar" *which documents that "when the Allauddin Khilji (An Afghan Turkish origin and second ruler of the Khilji dynasty in India (1295-1316AD) captured the City of Kambayat at the head of the gulf of Combay. He killed the adult male Hindu inhabitants for the glory of Islam, set flowing rivers of blood, sent women of the country with all the gold, silver and* *jewels to his **own home** and made about twenty thousand Hindu maidens on private slaves and victimized them **with the lust of both** Allauddin and his army chiefs."*

India has deep long cultural history, Hinduism began their culture around 1500BC and Buddhism around 600BC. The culture had evolved impossessive intellectual, religious and artistic pursuits. Pre and post the early days of Islam, Indian Scholars took their works in Science, Math's Zero AL zebra, geometry, the decimal system so called "Arabic" numbers but they are actually Hindu one. They have taken away the literature of Medicine and Philosophy to their courts including Baghdad)

Rizwan Salim (1997) writes what "the Arab really did". *Being savages at a very low level of civilization and no culture worth the name from Arabia and West Asia, began entering India from the early century onwards. Islamic invaders demolished countless Hindu Temples, innumerable forts and palaces of Hindu Kings, killed vast numbers of Hindu men and carried off Hindu women as slaves but many Indians do not seem to recognize that the alien Muslim had carried off Hindu women ...but many Indians do not seem to recognize that the alien Muslim Invaders destroyed the historical evolution of the earth's most intellectually advanced civilization and the most vigorously creative society Cited in Khan Page 179).*

"It appears that the Invaders have followed their prophets deeds who and when "**the steps taken by their Prophet was once a refugee (yathrib) taken by the Jewish Medina. Within 5 years he had driven out executed or enslaved every Jew there at**"

*Likewise the Invaders back stabbed their **hosts** and plundered the wealth, women, and Men children of their yathrib (shelter –Hosts). It is however reasonable to say that Indians of Pre-Islam fought many wars including Kurukhsetra, Panipat wars Rajput wars, **Indians never plundered their personal wealth** or beheaded all the soldiers of Islamic army, when they were defeated.*

*Battles were usually conducted on open soil between Military personnel. There was no concept of booty and this ideology was already put in their practice and hence Hindu Kings were **unprepared** for the ghastly acts of onslaught by Muslims. Not only India but the world (save Muslim) community followed the same method and planning in battlefield when they wage war. Indigenous Indian were forced to flee to jungles mountains face grueling exploitation and taxes slaughter or enslavement while their Society was demeaned and destroyed. Muslim constantly attacked the indigenous idolater population and also fought against each other in ceaseless revolts by generals, chiefs and princes during the tenure of Islamic rule.*

Slavery: Initially India included part of today's Pakistan (Sindh) Bangladesh, Bengal and Kashmir Hinduism and Buddhism flourished in Afghanistan during pre-Islamic intrusions (7th century and earlier) Further 16th century Afghanistan war divided between Muslim (Moghul) empire of India and the Safavids of Persia.

Initially the godless Umayyad's allowed Hindus a Dhimmis status. Possibly because of their large number, resistance to Asians and their value as a sources of Tax income. This violates Islamic text and law which demands death or conversion for idolaters and polytheists. When sultan Iltumush (D.1236) was asked why Hindus were given the choice between death and Islam he replied "***but at that time in India… the Muslims are so few that they are like salt in large dish)*** however after few years when Muslims are well established and the troops are no longer …it would be possible to give Hindus the choice of death or Islam (cited in Lal.c. p.538)"

Readers pleas pay your attention to the above quote.

It is often actual numbers are not given just comments like countless captives/slaves or all the women and children were taken where numbers are to take "where numbers are recorded they are terrifying along with people , the Muslim took everything that could coins, clothes, furniture idols, animals grains etc. were destroyed.

Muslim Rulers were foreigners: Until the 13th Century, most slaves were sent out of India but following the Sultanate of Delhi (1206) sold in India or sent elsewhere and slaves from elsewhere were imported and Muslims were composed of wide array of foreign slave groups converted to Islam and Hindus "the Indian converters." A sort slave *exchange business* was being run as trade after Spice trade, since, now they need to purchase the *spices* but they can plunder them from the produces.

Slaves were the promised booty from Allah and obtaining them was a strong motivation for Jihad.

"Slaves were so plentiful that they became very cheap men... were degraded but this is the goodness of Allah who bestows honors on his own religion and degrades infidelity {Muslim Chronicle Arabian Sultan Subuktajn of Ghazni slave Raid (942) in "Blood Soaked Hero")

The Ghajinavids-Turkish from Ghazni, Afghanistan (992-1206) who subdued Punjab. From 17 raids (pp7-1030) Sultan Mahmud Ghazni (Afghan name for Ghaznavi) resulting in the loss about two million people via slaughter or enslaved and sold outside. India (Khan P.35) Chroniclers (e.g. Utbi, the Sultan's Secretary) provides same number (From Thanesar), the Muslim Army brought 200,000 captives back to Ghazni (Afghanistan) in 1019, 53,000 were taken. At one time the Caliphs 1/5th share was 150,000 suggesting 750,000 captives 500,000 were taken in one campaign (Fatwa-Hind Lal©P.551) swords flashed like lighting amid the blackness of clouds and fountains of blood flowed like fall of setting star.

The friends of God defeated their opponents... the Musalman weakened and vengeance on the infidel the infidel enemies of god Killing 15000 making them food of the beasts and birds of prey...god also bestowed on his friends such an amount of bloody booty as was beyond and calculations including 5000,000 slaves beautiful men and women (Khan P.191)

Under the Ghaurivid (Turks) for example Muhammad Ghour (Afghan) and his Military Commander the ruler Qutubuddin Aibak (1206-1210) the Sultanate was setup. Mass beheading, enslavement forced conversion, plunder, and destruction of temples. Slaves were incredibly plentiful. In 1195 Aibak took 20,000 slaves from Raja Bhim and 50,000 at Kalinjar (1202) {Lal © p.536}. Even poor Muslim house holder became owner of numerous slaves (Khan 103-Lal © 537).

Through the 13/14th Century ruled by the Khilji and Tughlaq slavery grew as Islam spread. Thousands of slaves were sold at a low price every day (Khan P.280). Allauddin Khilji (1296-1316) capture of slaves was stupendous and the shackled, chained and humiliated slaves (Lal © p.540) in the sack of Somnath alone" he took the captive a great number of handsome and elegant maidens amounting to 20,000 and of both sexes…More than *pen can enumerate.* The Mohammadans army brought the country to utter ruin destroyed the lives of inhabitants and plundered the cities and captured off-springs (Historian cited i Boston p 641 {c) p.540"

Many thousands massacred Allauddin Khilji (129-1316) had 50,000 slave boys in his personal service, 70,000 slaves worked continuously on his buildings (Lal © p.541) The Sufi Amir Khusroo notes "**The Turks whenever they please, can sell or buy Hind** (Lal© p.541)

Eunuchs: All over the Islamic world, the conquered were castrated, including in India. This was done so that men could guard harems, provide carnal indulgence for the rulers, give devotion to the rulers as they had no hope of a family of their own and of course this quickly reduced the breeding of stock of the conquered. Castration was a common practice throughout Muslim rule possibly contributing to the Decline in India's population from 200 million in 1000CE to 170 million in 1500AD (CE Khan p.314) the Main purpose of nurturing Eunuchs is to look after the wives of Rulers so that the uncastrated slaves would prove risk in spoiling their harem sexually. Another reason is when once castrated he is unfit to produce children of their own thus the growth of Hindu population would be curtailed. Simply killing the all Hindus doesn't serve the purpose of their being Rulers and kings as they require slaves to work for the guarding both their lives along with their harems.

Once Sultan Bakhtiayar Khilji conquered Bengal in 1205, it became a leading supplier of castrated slaves. This remained with the case of into Moghul (1526-1857)

Akbar the great (1556-1605) owned Eunuchs said Khan Chagatai owned 1200 eunuchs (an official of Akbar's son Jahangir)! Aurangzeb reign in 1639 at Golkonda (Hyderabad) 22000 boys were emasculated and given to Muslim Rulers and governors on sale (Khan 313).

Sultan Allauddin Khilji (1296-1316) had 50,000 boys in his personal service. Sultan Mohammad Tughlaq (1325-1388CE) had 20,000 and Sultan Feroz Tughlaq (1351-1388) had 40,000. (Feroz Tughlaq liked to collect boys in any way and had 180,000 slave in total (Lal © p.542). Several Commanders under various Sultanates were eunuchs, Muslim historians record that infatuation of Sultan Mahamud Ghazni, Qutubuddin Aibak and Sikandar Lodi for handsome young boys! Sultan Mahmoud was infatuated by his Hindu Commander Tilak (Khan.314)

Conclusion: The in human behavior applied to the whole Indian population by Muslims was the same whether Muslims were Sufis, Arabs, Afghans, Turks of Moghul as all followed Islam's laws text and the examples of Mohammad. Prophet Muhammad in the Hadith of Bukhari has clearly stated that "For us killing and castration of the male and converting women as booty or slaves to satisfy our carnal desires as our Lord Allah has granted this kind of activity for Muslims while waging war" (Khan© p.543)

It should also be noted that the violence and destruction, plunder, slaughter and enslavement continued even after they had virtual control over India because the aim was not merely to conquer but to force all into Islam and procure slaves, as was being done with Africans. Muslim did not come to India for trade but they came to wipe out and replace it with Islam- which tells them that they own everything of the default because it is the booty promised by Allah. **The pagans/idolaters and polytheists had to convert or die and only then there could there be Peace** *with Islam in the World and Slaves were the reward for Islamic fighters-part of the booty promised by Allah.*

CHAPTER 7

EUROPEAN ENTRY FURTHERED THE STING OF INFLAMMATION

As we studied about deeds of democide on native Hindus in earlier sections of the treatise, Aurangzeb was unlikely Moghul Hero. He believed that he had divine desperation to rule, not for his own enjoyment of power, but for the restoration of True Kingdom of Islam in India. Characteristically when his sister Jahanara pleased with him to spare the life of brother DaraShikon and for that "Dara is an Infidel and a friend of Hindus. He must extirpated for the sake of true faith and peace of the realm. He had no feeling for his father either, and in all the years he kept him confined in the Agra Fort, he never once visited him, not even during his final illness, and did not attend his funeral also. He had already killed his two elder brothers to take over the Power. He had no weakness of sentiment or love.

Under Aurangzeb the very nature of Moghul Empire changed. Shahjehan had tentatively begun the conversion of the secular empire into a theoretical Muslim State, the process was now completed by Aurangzeb. He re-imposed Jizya, 115 years after Akbar, abolished it and imposed disabilities on Non- Muslims as required by orthodox Islamic tradition.

In the first Phase Aurangzeb life ended in 1681, after returning from North India to begin with final ascent to the summit of Moghul Empire. He spent his next 20 years there in ceaseless wars, campaigning new territories subduing rebels, capturing Forts. At the end of this Titanic effort, a vast sweep of land from Kabul across virtually the entire Indian sub-continent lay under his away. These are no more lands to conquer, no more forts to take or armies to defeat. He became the master of the largest empire that India has ever known.

Mughal imperial destiny had been filled it seemed. Yet, just then Aurangzeb appeared absolutely triumphant, everything was in fact utterly lost. At the moment of his supreme triumph, Aurangzeb found to his horror that the very ground on which he stood was crumbling.

The Marathas were his nemesis. Aurangzeb thought that he had pounded them into the earth and indeed he had, but he rose again after the death of Shivaji, Marathas rose again out of the soil everywhere to confound him, when the weary old Emperor began his slow trek north wards to Delhi his mission "accomplished", the Marathas hounded him, incessantly snapping at his heels. Meanwhile seeing the Emperor's helplessness, Panic began to spread through the Empire, and the immense mutilated Moghul administrative edifice began to crack and crumble. Rebels and bandits roamed the land freely as Aurangzeb's sons, even grandsons squared off to fight for the succession. Aurangzeb budged on. But on the way while campaigning at Ahmed Nagar in central Maharashtra, he fell ill with high fever. On3 March 1707, while he was saying his prayers, Aurangzeb, 89 years old and Indian Emperor for 49 years slid into death. He had once said "Az mast Hamah fasad-i-baqi that after me chaos.

As a result of his death, several local powers of Jats, Sikh, Ahirs, Marathas, and Rohillas attempted to exercise power in a manner that involved and affected much larger population of India. Not only that there was much mutual rivalries and conflicts among these powers as they were keen to set up their in independent Kingdoms of Pocket influence. The fall of Mughal Emperor gave Indian Hindu a great sigh of relief.

The Mogul Empire faced very serious problems on all fronts. The war of succession among his three sons ensued that several weakness the Moghul Empire. There had been some *fourteen Moghul emperors after Aurangzeb to Bahadur Shah Zafar*, the last Moghul Emperor. Several of them served only titular head of the Moghul Empire most of them were indolent, dissolute and incompetent rulers in capable of evoking either respect or fear. They were always busy in their luxuries, opulence and intrigues and nothing to remedy, the evils that had crept into Moghul polity.

(B) EUROPEAN INTRUDERS:

In the name of *Spice Trade*, the Europeans entered India and started colonization of India and its subordination to British Empire. Of the early European colonies, the Portuguese seems to symbolize best of the total disregard; it will and destructive of the West towards India. Whatever all the folklores today about the relaxed atmosphere of Portuguese Goa (the Good life, the wine, and women) the Portuguese were ruthless lot. In 1498 Vasco da Gama the Portuguese Hero was generously received by Zamorin the Hindu King of Calicut who granted him the right to establish ware house (for spices) obtained patent rights from the King for commerce. But once Hindu tolerance was exploited and the Portuguese wanted more. In 1510 Alfonso de Albuquerque seized Goa where he stated a reign of terror burning "heretic's" crucifying the Brahmins, using false theories too forcibly to convert the lower, castles and encouraging his soldiers to take Indian Mistresses. Indeed the inquisition in Goa had nothing to envy the Muslim except in sheer number. Ultimately the Portuguese had to be kicked out of India when all other colonies had already left.

British India came India during 1600's. They came to India as Spice Traders, and they did not harbor any political ambitions. Slowly they extended the trade to various parts of India and several British officials had started residing for a long time in the country. As such they started building factories which stationed British officials and several British soldiers with permission of the local Nobles and Rulers. This ensured that a political upheaval against the Rulers would not affect the British.

The equation changed with French. Although they also arrived as Traders, the French Governor General Joseph-Francois

Dupleix dreamed of French Empire in the sub-continent. He started French Empire in the sub-continent. He started favoring Kings taking sides in the battles and if the supported side won, he used to demand greater Power for the French. This emerged the British and also adopted the French modus operendi, soon military and Economic powers but shunned complete take over the Kingdom and administrative responsibility. East India Company now realized that the divide and policy could easily be controlled by them. With policies and politics it started to take over the Kingdoms on different pretext fights for the throne by the (princely states) like **absence of the son of the king**, inability of the king to provide tributes). Finally after the 1857 revolt the crown assumed responsibility of Indian Empire that Military victory apart the British in India was impossible and people had to accept the new rules. British became largest empire after taking over the power on India from Moghul in the World that a saying was used up to "**The sun never sets on the British Empire**. Under the policies of British colonist, people around the globe were subjected to mass famines atrocious conditions in concentrated camps and brutal massacre at the hands of imperial troops.

The British also played an integral role in the **transatlantic trade**. Things began to change after the arrival of Gandhi in the political scenario. He began mass movement, a new strategy of moral invasion, against the British and India won Freedom and finally became an Independent India in 1947. It is however, is a time to know what horrors the British imposed on Indians is dealt the following sections.

The occasion when the East India Comp[any received its charter from the Queen Elizabeth, to 1947, Mountbatten pack up the Union Jack, the History of British in India has been one of the **subtle treachery gross commercial exploitation and sometimes of savagery. The English might have been totally ignorant India's past greatness, when the set up acquiring bit by bit their empire, but at least there was some early attempt at understanding each other between the enlightened British** *and some Indians.* But after Mutiny of 1857, the English went to frenzy of murders, revenge and atrocity and alienated themselves for even from the natives. Henceforth they would live separately in their effort in their forts or in their cantonments and would be totally segregated from Indians, ending forever any chance of bridging the gap between the cultures. Indeed Danieou feels that the revolt "was to trigger the slow and insidious destruction of one greatest civilization of the world its philosophy its art, its sciences and its techniques now despised and discouraged. This was ward disaster for universal culture, he concluded (History de I'nde Page 329)

British divided India they exploited schism between Hindus and Muslims and aggregated a small discontentment in Sikh community. Dividing a small discontent in Sikh community. Dividing India them was only a practical need to further their imperial dream. It was not done out of sheer financial conviction. Their first prey was Adivasis the tribal people which they promptly proceeded to the name as *"original inhabitants of India who were colonized by the dirty Brahmins during the mythical Aryan invasion"* Was it no right they said to free them from the grip of their masters who had enslaved them both socially and religiously.

That was how they set the Adivasis against the main stream of Hindu Society and *sowed the seeds of an explosive conflict* is exploited politically by politicians like Mulayam singh Kanshi Ram or Laloo Prasad. The Missionaries were always supporters of colonialism, they encouraged it and their whole structure was based on "the good western civilized world being brought to the Pagans. In the words of Charles Grant (1746-1823) of the East India Company: "We cannot avoid recognizing in the people of Hindustan and a race of men lamentably degenerate base, governed by Malevolent and licentious passion and shrunk in Misery by their vices". Claudius Buchanan a chaplain attached to the East India Company, went even further....neither truth nor honesty, honesty, for our gratitude nor charity is to be found in the breast of a Hindu ." Thus is the comment about a nation that gave the world the Vedas and the Upanishads, at the time when European were still formicating in their caves.

Lord Hasting, governor General of India from 1813 could not agree more; he writes in his diary on October 2nd of the year that *"the Hindu appears a being nearly limited to animal functions...with no higher intellect than a dog or elephant or a monkey..."* No wonder that the British opened the doors wide to missionaries.

Such was the case with Pondicherry Adivasis to whom French lured to cut of their lives from the main stream of Hinduism India.

Missionaries abort Adivasis cultural roots and the life them who trusted British and started worshiping the Christ as God when British Masters never looked after them after conversion. Now they are looked and termed as Anglo-Indians, a race which became neither here nor there. Hence they had slowly disappear, either reverting to their Indian-ness or settling abroad, but evolution does not tolerate the people that loses its self-identity.

Likewise another European Country that is French-India adopted the same deal with "Pondicherry's". French Tamil origin from Pondicherry. They originated from lower castes they were converted by the French missionaries and in time assumed French names, French manners and considered themselves as French. But today the French have forgotten them; they cost too much to their Government and apart from few brilliant exceptions, they are also a race which is slowly dying and is gradually engulfed by the Indian Tamils. It is also true that the Missionaries such as Saint Francoise Xavier broke down many idol temples to build their churches.

Koenaraad Elst writes that "the missionaries were ultimately all set to trigger Christian partition of India; at the time of Independence Christian Mission centers had dreamed upon plan for Christian in collaboration of Muslim League. The far North-East *Chotanager and parts of Kerala the Hub House of*

Spices were to become Christian States, forming Non-Hindu chain with Nizam Hyderabad and with Pakistan Bengal. The secret agreement between the Muslim League and Missionaries acting as "Representatives of Tribal interest is some time used in Muslim propaganda as a proof that *Muslim and Tribal are natural allies.*"

It was however who foiled their plans (indigenous India page 229)

Even the independence the Missionaries seem to have been involved sectionalist activities in India's North East as well as Burmese side of the Border. Always pretending to act as *mediators* they appear to have actually helped the separatists with vital information since then they have been indicting the policies Nagaland, Meghalaya and Mizoram, which recently celebrated with great fanfare its century of Christian Rule.

C. MISREPRESENTATION OF INDIAN HISTORY BY INVADERS AND MISSIONERIES:

Before the inception of Monotheistic religion both Arabs and romans were barbarians and savage. Almost all the Abrahamic Religions practiced Monotheism. It was Jews that have started by saying that their God Yahweh has created Universe and while creating Universe he created Man, Earth, Animals, Sun Moon and stars within Six and days and there cannot be another God and there's is only one God as ascertained in Old Testament. Christians and Muslims while barrowing this Monotheistic view from Jews they declared their own Holy Books of New Testament by Christians and Quran by Muslims. Though the Concept of these books is the same, they manipulated their scriptures with some additions and alterations and claimed that their books are original including their Gods. On account of these revised concept they fought each other. Millions to billions were slaughtered in the name of crusades and the wars in the name of Terrorism are being still continued. Muslims adopted sword method in spreading their religion in the whole world. Christians stopped their crusades and finally they started continuing the spread of their Religion thorough Missionaries.

The History of Arabs and Romans speaks about their barbaric attitude before the inception of their religion. Both of them rendered much harm to other developed civilization like India and Egypt. Egypt along with most of the African counties however fell prey to the Muslims and Christians. Finally they entered India in the name of *spice trade* started crusades, one by sword method and another by Missionary method. Both of them fetched the Crown of India one after another. Millions of natives of India that is Hindus, Buddhists and Jains were grounded and out of the residual population major portion of Hindus were made either their slaves or servants on receiving the payment of Jizya Tax which is meant to live in their own country as citizens of India till they obtained Independence in 1947 through the method non-violent resistance.

C. Desecration in India: It is said that India was the Jewel in the crown in of the British Empire East India company began making into the subcontinent in the 17th Century and India was established in 1858.

(A) British Raj systematically transferred the wealth of the region into their own coffers. In the north eastern region of Bengal, the first great ideal industrialization of the Modern world occurred.

(B) The prosperous two centuries old weaving Industry was shut down after the British flooded to local market with the cheap fabric from northern England. India still grew cotton, but the Bengali population no longer spun it and the weavers became it and the weavers became beggars.

(C) India suffered around a dozen major famines, under British Rule with an estimated 12 to 29 million starving death.

(D) Orissa famine occurred in North Eastern India in 1866 over million or one in third local people perished. As the regions Textiles Industry was destroyed more people were pushed into agriculture and were dependent on the monsoon.

(E) When British finally got out of India they simply drew a line down the map and portioned the subcontinent into India and Pakistan. The more lead to the mass migration of the people around 10 million people and when it escalated into sectarian violence an estimated one million lost their lives.

(F) In 1943, a deadly famine swept in Bengal region of modern East India and Bangladesh. Between one and three million people died in tragedy that was completely preventable. At the time of extent of suffering they were busy dealing with a war to look after its empire properly.

*Winston Churchill the Prime Minister of British **refused to divert to supplies** away from already well supplied British troops saying the war effort would not allow it. This would not be too damned but at the same time blocked American and Canadian ships from delivering aid to India either. Nor would he allow the Indians to help themselves: the colonial Government forbade the country from using its own ships for currency resolves to hold the starving masses. Meanwhile, London pushed up the price of grain with hugely inflated purchases making it unaffordable for the dying and destitute. Most chillingly of all when the Government of Delhi telegrammed to tell the people were dying, Churchill allegedly replied to **ask why Gandhi had not yet died"***

D. ABUSE OF INDIA'S PAST BY EUROPEAN WHILE WRITING HISTORY

(i)The Invasion of Aryans over Dravidians: The British missionaries wrote our Indian History and documented false events of to make us believe. The theory of invasion is till taken as the foundation stone of our Indian History. In accordance their theory, which was devised during 18th and 19th century by British linguist and Archaeologists, the first inhabitants of India were dark good-natured and peaceful dark skinned shepherds called the Dravidians who founded what is called Harappa or

Indus Valley Civilization. There were supposedly remarkable builders witness the Mohenjo-Daro Harappa in Pakistani Sind, but had no culture to speak off, no literature and improper script even. The around 1500Bc Aryans said to have invaded India. The Aryans were of white skinned, nomadic people, who originate somewhere in Western Russia and imposed Dravidian upon the hateful caste system. To the Aryans are attributed Sanskrit, the Vedic or Hindu Religion. Both Vedas and Upanishads and mythological writings of Mahabharata and Ramayana.

It is however to say that it is a kind of a 'master stroke' on the part of British as said by Francois Gautier. To speak truth they have cited with two tongues; one side ancient civilization was not that old and on the other tongue Western world that is Mesopotamia, Samaria and Babylonia whatever good things India had developed like Sanskrit, literature and even architecture had been influenced by the West. Thus Sanskrit, instead of being the Mother of Indo-European languages became the just a branch of their huge family, the religion of Zaurashtra is said to have influenced Hinduism and not vice versa. On the other hand it divided India and pitted against each other the low caste dark skinned Dravidians and high caste light skinned ?Aryans, a rift which is still enduring.

It is however, a known fact that this theory is being challenged by two new discoveries one archaeological and the other the Linguistic. Firstly in the Rig-Veda the Ganges, India's sacred River is only mentioned once, but the mythic Saraswathi is praised around fifty times. For a long time the Saraswathi River was indeed considered a myth, until the America's **Landsat** was able to photograph the source in the Himalayas. Archaeologist Paul Henri Frankfort who studied the Saraswathi region at the beginning of nineties found out that the Saraswathi had disappeared because around 2200 B.C.

On account of immense draught reduced the whole region to aridity and famine. Thus he writes most inhabitants moved away from the Saraswathi to settle on the banks of Indus and Sutlej rivers". According to Official History, the Vedas were composed around 1500 BC some even say 1200 BC. Yet the Rig-Veda describes India as it was before the great drought which dried up the Saraswathi, which means the effect that the so called Indus or Harappa Civilization was a continuation of the Vedic Epoch, which ended approximately when the Saraswathi was dried up.

Recently the famous ***Indus seals*** discovered at the site of Mohenjo-Daro and Harappa have been reportedly deciphered by Dr. Jha, a distinguished linguist. In the biased light of the Aryan invasion theory the seals were presumed to be written in a crude Harappa (read Dravidian) script although they had never been convincingly deciphered. But according to Raja Ram and Jha "the Harappa civilization, of which the ***seals are a product belonged to the later part of Vedic Age.*** It had close connections with Vedantic works like the Sutras and the Upanishads. The style of writings reflects the short aphorisms found in Sutra works. The imagery and symbolism are strongly Vedic. The vocabulary depends heavily upon the Vedic glossary Nighantu and is commented by Yaksha known as the Nirukla. The name Yaksha is found on at least two seals or possibly three. These are references to Vedic Kings and sages as well place names of particular interest are references to ***plaksharga*** or the birth place of Saraswathi River and ***sapta apah*** or the land of the Seven Rivers.

This proves authoritatively that the Rig Veda must have already have been quite ancient by the time the Harappa Civilization. Since the Harappa civilization was known to have been in existence by 4000 BC. This contention is now receives the archaeological support following RS Bish's investigation of the great Harappa city of Dholavira, Bishi (another archaeologist have concluded that the Vedic Aryans of the Saraswathi heart land and were the people who created the Harappa cities and the civilization associated with. In this Connection Aurobindo, Indian greatest yogi, poet Philosopher also supported this theory (In his India's Rebirth-page 103) He wrote that Indian History required to be rewritten.

(ii) The second abused information is the Caste System. Secondly the caste system has been the most misunderstood, the most vilified subject of Hindu society at the hands of Western Historians and even today by the secular Indians. To understand the original purpose behind the caste system one must go back to the Vedas. Cast was originally an arrangement for the distribution of functions in Society, just as much as class in Europe, but the principle on which this distribution was based was peculiar to India. A Brahmanism was a Brahmin and not by mere birth, but because he discharged the function or duty of prescribing the spiritual and intellectual elevation of race, and he had to cultivate the spiritual temperament and acquire the spiritual training which along would qualifying him for the last.

Similarly Kshatriya not merely because he was son of warriors who safeguard the society from the foreign invasions. He destined to protect the Country. It is therefore his duty is to preserve high voltage of energy like a lofty Samurai and this he has to cultivate the princely temperament. Thirdly Vaishya whose function was to amass wealth for the race/country and the Sudra who discharged humbler duties without which the other classes could not perform their share of labor for the common good (Aurobindo In India's Rebirth)

Many other sages have gone beyond Aurobindo arguing that the occult relation India had with Universal force, each one was bot in caste corresponding to his/her spiritual evolution. No they might be some accidents, misfits, errors they say but the system seems to have worked pretty well until modern times of materialism and Western influence.

(iii) The third misnomer is about Vedas: the third piece of disinformation concerns Vedic Religion. Danieou, maintains that original Vedas were a moral Dravidian tradition which was reshaped by the Aryans and later put down in Sanskrit. He finds lineage between Vedic religion and Persian religion (Zarathustra) as well as the Greek Gods the problem is that he seem to imply that the Vedas Religion may have sprung from Zoroastrian creed! He also puts down all Vedic Symbols as purely physical signs for instance Agni is the fire that should always bur in the houses altar. Finally he sees in Rig Veda "Only a remarkable document on the mode of life the society and history of the Aryan (Histoire I'nde Page 62)

This theory appears like cock and bull story. Actual abuse of information started again with the missionaries who saw in the Vedas the root of the Evil", the source of Paganism and went systematically about belittling it. Even they have gone to the extent of telling that Vedas are only 1500-1000 BC. But it is known factor that during period of Aryans that is 5000 BC back the Vedas were written and these are and linguistic Analyzers support this fact. Vedas do contain almost all the Scientific, Philosophical, Religious, clinical, dynamics, decimal system, Zero and Algebra, Sale and measurement systems were included as detailed in earlier chapter. Readers please note this point.

CHAPTER 8

SEPOY MUTINY AND INDEPENDENCE MOVEMENT

Indian Mutiny also called Sepoy Mutiny wide spread but unsuccessful rebellion against British Rule in India in 1857-58. Begun in Meerut by Indian troops (Sepoy) in the Service of British East India Company, it spread in Delhi, Agra, Kanpur and Lucknow. In India is officially called as the first war of Independence and other similar names.

Indian Rebellion of 1857: To regard the rebellion as a Sepoy Mutiny is to underestimate the root cause leading to it British paramountcy that is belief in British dominance in Indian political Economic and cultural life had been introduced in India about 1820. The British increasingly used *a variety of tactics* to usurp control of the Hindu Princely states that were under what were called subsidiary alliances with the British everywhere

in old Indian aristocracy was being replaced by British officials. One notable British technique was called the *doctrine of lapse* first perpetuated by Lord Dalhousie in 1840's: It involved the British prohibiting a Hindu ruler without a natural hair from adopting successor and after the ruler the growing discontent of the Brahmans many of who had been dispossessed of their reverences or had lost lucrative positions.

Another serious concern was the increasing pace of Westernization ideas. Missionaries were challenging the religious beliefs of the Hindus. The Humanitarian Movement led to reforms that went deeper the political super structure. During his tenure as a Governor General of India (1848-56) Lord Dalhousie made efforts toward emancipating women and had *introduced a bill to remove all legal obstacles to the remarriage of Hindu Widows, converts to Christianity* were to share with their Hindu relatives in the property of the family estate. There was a widespread belief that the British methods of education was a direct challenge to Orthodoxy, both Hindu and Muslims.

The Mutiny broke out in the Bengal Army because only in the military sphere that Indians were organized on the pretext for revolt was the introduction of the new Enfield rifle. To load it the Sepoys' has a bite of the ends of lubricated cartridges. The fact of information spread *among the Sepoy that the grease used to lubricate the Cartridge was mixture of pigs and cows lard;* thus to have oral contract with it was insult to both Muslims and Hindus. However the perception that the Cartridge were tainted added to the larger suspicion that British were trying to undermine Indian traditional society. For their part, the British did not pay enough attention to the growing level of Sepoy discontent.

The Revolt: In the late March 1857 a Sepoy named Mangal Pandey attacked British Officers at the Military garrison in Barrackpore. Later he was arrested Mutiny garrison in early April. Later in April the Mutiny trappers at Meerut refused the Enfield cartridges and as punishment they were giving a long prison terms fettered and put in Jail. This punishment incensed their comrades who rose on May 10, shot their British Officers and marched to Delhi where there were no European troops. There the local Sepoy garrison joined the Meerut men and by nightfall the aged pensionary Moghul Emperor Bahadur Shah Jaffar II had been nominally restored to power by tumultuous solidarity. The seizure of Delhi provided a focus and set the pattern for a whole mutiny which then spread and his sons and Nana Sahib the adopted son of the deposed son of Maratha Peshwas, none of the important princes joined the Mutineers.

From the time of the Mutineers' seizure of Delhi, the British operations to suppress the mutiny were divided into three parts. First came the desperate struggle at Delhi, Kanpur and Lucknow during the Summer then the operations around Lucknow in the winter 1857-58 directed by sir Hugh Rose in early 1858. Peace war officially declared on July 18, 1858. A grim future of the Mutiny was the ferocity that accompanied it. The Mutineers commonly shot their British officers on rising and were responsible for Massacre at Delhi Kanpur and elsewhere. The murder of women and children enraged the British, but in fact some British officers began to take severe measures before they knew that any such murders had occurred. In the end of the reprisals far outweighed the original excesses. Hundreds of Sepoys' were bayoneted or fired from cannons in fringy of British vengeance through some British Officer did the bloodshed.

Aftermath: the immediate result of the Mutiny was general house cleaning of the Indian administration. This East India Company was abolished in favor of the direct rule of India by British Government. In concentrate terms this did not mean much, but it introduced a more personal note into the government and removed the unimaginative commercialism that had lingered in the court of Directors. The financial crisis caused by the Mutiny led to reorganization.

Indian administrative system: Army was extensively reorganized. Another significant result of the mutiny was the beginning of policy consultation with Indians. The legislation council of 1853 had contained only Europeans and arrogantly behave as if it were full-fledged parliament. It was accorded by the new council of 1861 was given an Indian an Indian-nominated element. The educated and Public Programs (roads, railways, telegraph and Irrigation) continued with little interpretation; in fact some were stimulated by thought of their value for transport of troops in a crisis. Finally there was the effect of the mutiny on the people of India themselves.

Traditional society had made its protest against the incoming alien influences and it had failed. The princes and other natural leaders had either held aloof from mutiny or had proved the most part in competent. From this time all serious hope of a revival of the past or an exclusion of the West diminished. The traditional structure of Indian Society began to break down and was eventually suppressed by Westernized class system, from which emerged a strong middle class with a heightened sense of Indian Nationalism.

The Forgotten brutality of 1857 Mutiny highlighted:

A 160 year old skull of Sepoy Alam Beg, no in the possession of the Irish Historian Dr. Kim Wagner, now in London is a one of the glaring proof that colonial rulers who brought many modern inventions and practices to India were also is ***most inhuman***.

Head Hunting is usually associated with primitive tribes and contemporary terrorists, but the colonial rulers of India also collected heads of the Indian soldiers as war trophies.

In 1857, Alam Beg also known as Alum Bheg was a soldier with the 46th Bengal Native Infantry, an arm of the East India Company. The Mutiny of 1857 was crushed mercilessly and many gruesome incidents of that Era find mention in official records. In 2014 around the time when Mr. Wagner began writing his book on Alam Bheg, Ajmal in Punjab's Amritsar hit the headlines when authorities discovered skeleton of 282 soldiers who were executed after the Mutiny. They apparently had a surrounded hoping for a fair trial, but the Deputy Commissioner of the District Frederick henry Cooper ordered execution of the rebels. They were buried with medals and even money of the East India Company that many of them had in their pockets. The grisly discovery is yet to receive closure as the family of those soldiers remain untraced.

Similar is the condition of Alam Bheg has his journey back home remains in complete but Mr. Wagner believed that his only physical remain should find a proper peaceful burial. The Historian sad that the "absence of the descendants of such soldiers, it is the Indian Government that should bring back Alum Bheg to his mother land."

Head hunting by colonial's rulers from Europe was a rampant practice in the 19th century and activists Worldwide have been vocal in demanding human remains from Western Museums and collectors should be returned to their Countries of Origin.

There are no longer any records for Sepoys' of the Bengal Army- the best I could do was locate the area where 46ᵗʰ regiment recruited from, Mr. Wagner said.

Few tit bit though they appear but radical information how British took measures to put an end to this rebellion which include:

- By the beginning of 6 of May, 1857 the Delhi, Meerut, Rohil Khand Agra, Allahabad and Banaras divisions had been placed under Martial Law.
- By series of Acts Passed in May and June the definition of martial law was enlarged Martial Law.
- All restriction on the use of Power were removed.
- One Officer wrote to The Times: "We have the power of Life and death in our hands and I assure you we spare not. A very summary trial is all that takes place.
- Any form of rebellion from stealing to desertion and posseting money that could not be accounted for was punished by death.
- Imperial Rule could only be maintained and reproduced by a show of terror and force. ***The fiction of civilizing the Indian dissolved in the reality of the violence***.
- Colonel James Neil who was one of the community office of the troops that moved up the Gangetic Plain to quell the

uprising gave the following orders to "Settle the town and the country around Allahabad "All men inhabiting there including villages were to be slaughtered.

- The town of Fatehpur which had revolted to be attacked and the Pathan quarters destroyed with their inhabitants. All heads of insurgents particularly at Fatehpur to be hanged
- All Sepoys' of Mutinous regiments not giving a good account of themselves were to be hanged.
- If Deputy Collector is taken, hang him and have head cut off and struck up on one of the Principal (Mohammedan) building and the town.
- Never before and never after in the History of British Rule in India was there violence at the level that 1857 witnessed (We have been studying the causes and failure of Sepoy Mutiny as informed by the British Historians which is totally misleading and cowardice statements) The British rule in North India had come perilously close to bring destroyed and British had no other instrument at their command except deployment of terror on a grand scale to restore their dominance. Their prime intention was to Imperial rule could only be maintained and reproduce by show of Terror and force: which gives wrong notion of the fiction of civilizing the Indian dissolved in the reality of the violence.

- William Howard Russell the correspondent of the London Times "Who was in India in 1858 met an officer who as a part of the column that under Neil's orders marched from Allahabad to Kanpur and reported that "Every Indian who appeared in sight was shot or hung on the trees that lined the road; villages were burnt. Tyranny thus confronted rebellions.
- The officer reported that "in two days 42 men were hanged on the road side and a batch of Men was executed because their face were turned the wrong way when they were met on the march.
- The Government was unofficially warned about the policy of burning village: it would make cultivation impossible, a famine inevitable and land revenue scarce. But there was a purpose in their action of arson.
- The burning of village's homesteads, human shelters, barns, crops and so on was aimed to interpret the solidarity and cycle of agriculture and that was the pivot of that form of life.
- A village is also a site of stories, myths and histories by burning it the British sought to obliterate the memory of a culture.

- Reflecting on these counter insurgency measures J.W Kaye who in the late 1860's and 1870' penned magisterial history of what he called the "***Sepoy War***" and he was not known to be sympathetic to the rebels wrote" over the whole of the Sepoy was there is no darker cloud than that which gather over Allahabad in this terrible summer… It is on the records of our British Parliament in Papers sent home by the Governor General of India in council that the "aged women and children are sacrificed as those guilty of rebellion. ***They were not deliberately hanged but burnt to death*** in the Villagestheir boasting in writing that they had **spared no one** and that peppering away at ***riggers was very pleasant pastime***. This mischievous act deliberately speaks of the fact that they want to create hate wall among Hindu Muslims and enjoy the colonial power to rule India for life time.

Time line of Independence movement:

Period	Progress of India's independent Movement
1857-1864- **1875-1876** **1882-1983-** **1885-1897**	(i)Sepoy Mutiny-**1857** (ii)Establishment of Scientific society by Syed Ahmed in **1864** (iii) Establishment of Theosophical Society and Establishment Indian League **1875 (iv)** Vernacular Press Act in **1876 (v)** Hander Commission (also known as Indian Education Commission in **1882 (vi)** Elbert Bill Passed -**1883-(vii)** Establishment of INC (First INC session was held at Bombay which was presided by W.C. Banerjee in **1885- (viii)** The Indian National congress launched in Bombay with the aim of winning political rights for Indians. **(ix)** Ramakrishna mission founded by Swami Vivekananda during**1897**
1905	The partition of Bengal leads to a massive upsurge among the people and a call for swadeshi goods, leading to boycott of British manufactured goods.
1906-1907- **1908-1909**	Formation of Muslim League. Congress given a call for Swaraj (ii) Execution of Khudiram Bose on 11th August 1908-(iii) Minto Marley Reforms (also called Indian Council Act-1909 (iv) 1907 – Surat split of INC16th October 1907)

1911	Bengal partition nulled announced that the capital of India from India to from Calcutta to Delhi
1916-1917	Lucknow Pact –(ii) Chaperon Satyagraha(1917) (iii)Lucknow pact reached between INC and Muslim league (1916)-Establishment of Home Rule by Balagangadhar Tilak
1914-1918	Britain drags India into World war I sixty thousand lose their lives in the first Great war
1919	The Khilafat Movement; 16th February 1919- and Montague chums Ford Reforms British seeks to introduce the Rowlett Act imposing severe curbs on civil rights. Indians protests peacefully. 13th April 1919-Massacre of Jallianwala Bag in Amritsar, 400 men and children who had gathered peacefully against the Act killed.
1920-	Non-cooperation Movement
1921-1922	Gandhi launches the Civil disobedience/Non-Cooperation movement calls for boycott of British goods. Calls off movement a year later due to Chauri-Choura killing where mob killed police men.
1923-1924-1925	Moplah riots between Hindus and Muslims ((**ii**) **1925** Kokoris conspiracy
1927-1928-1929	The British Government appoints the Simon Commission. The commission is boycotted when Visits India the following year (**ii**) on **8th April1929** Bombing in Central Legislative Assembly by Bhagat singh (**iii**) **December 8th 1929**-Lahore Session Poorna Swaraj declared) (**iv**) **3rdFebruary 1928** Simon commission arrives India (**iv**) **1928-*Assassination of Saunders by Bhagat Singh*** (**v**) 1928 –Nehru Report
1930	Gandhi leads **Salt Satyagraha (Dandi March)** to protest against the British government to amend the law. The congress boycott the ***First Round Table conference in London.(12th March Civil disobedience movement starts with Dandi March) (iii) Chittagong army raid.***

1931	**Second Round Table conference** leads to Gandhi **Irwin pact** that ends the rights to Indians on 5th March 1931 (ii) Karachi Session of INC (iii)Second Round Table Conference
1932 March	Gandhi concludes the **Poona Pact with Dr. Ambedkar** that does away with **separate electorate for Untouchables** but reserves some electoral seats for them. **(ii) Poona Act (iii) 3rd Round Table Conference**
1935	Government of India Act passed by the British and gives Indian **political rights at the provincial level.**
1937	Provincial election most provinces elect **Congress**, some elect **Muslims**.
1939-40	Outbreak of World War II. Viceroy unilaterally declared India's Participation in the War leading to congress ministries and the Congress boycotting the British in Protest. (ii) August Offer by Lord Lithgow 18 and 22 August) (All India forward Block Formed ON 22nd June 1939)
1941	SubashChandra Bose escapes from India to join hands with the Axis Powers against the British.
1942-March	The British was cabinet announces the Staffer Crips Mission to negotiate India's political status after the War.
1942-May	Gandhi meets Cripps but call his proposals a "postdated Cheque". Congress rejected the proposals.
1942-August	The Congress leader meet in Bombay and pass the **"Quit India"** Resolution calling for complete Independence from the British Rule. The congress leadership arrested; Gandhi is Jailed at the **Aga Khan Palace in Poona** for defying the British and called for Independence. (ii) Cripps Mission (ii) Establishment of Indian Independence League –(iii)Formulation of Azad Hind Fouz

1943	Bose taken charge of Indian National Army, begins march to India which is stopped outside **Imphal.**
1945	World War II ends and the Labor Party which is sympathetic to Wavell Plan and announced in Shimla -India's call for Independence, **forms Government**.
1946	Gandhi –Jinnah's talk fail-riots broke out. Cabinet Mission (formulated at the initiative of Clement Attlee PM of UK)
1947-June	The British, congress and Muslim League agree to partition and Independence as proposed by Mount Batten Plan—Indian Independence Act announced
1947-August 15	Indian Independence communal rights claim thousand and million in partition

CHAPTER 9

PARTITION AND ITS AFTERMATH

A. Some important shocking facts about partition that every Indian must know.

1. Cyril Radcliffe, the man who designed the border between the two nations arrived India a few days before partition and had no knowledge about anything except the geographical lay out of the country. Out of ignorance of the prevailing conditions he divided the country without any consideration of religious and cultural Communities, thus causing a rift between Hindus and Muslims.

2. The Indian Government had estimated that about 14.5 million people would be displaced during Partition. The partition caused the largest mass migration inhuman History.

3. Every one wonder why Pakistan got Independence on the 14th and India on the 15th of August 1947? Mount Batten wanted personally attended both Pakistan and India's Independence ceremony (this would not have possible had both the countries gained Independence on the same day.

4. The Father of the Nation Gandhi was not present in Delhi during the Partition. Instead he was in Calcutta on August 15 1947, where he prayed confronted riots and worked with Hussein Shaheed Suharwardy to stop communal killing. He owed the day of Independence fasting and spinning.

5. Even though both Pakistan and India achieved Independence on by 14th and 15th August respectively, it was not until the *17th August* there was an announcement of border between two countries.

6. In early 1947 it was decided that the partition will be carried on the 3rd of June 1958. The British Prime Minister clement

Atlee announced that Britain would leave India no later than June 1948.

7. Astrologer were consulted to take out an appropriate date for the event midnight of august 15th was decided.

8. The Princely state Jammu and Kashmir had not decided which side to join by August 15th 1947. Pakistan believed that Jammu and Kashmir should belong to their side since it housed a large number of Muslims. However, the Hindu Maharaja finally agree to join Indian in October 1947.

9. After the partition, Pakistan got 1/3 of the Indian Army 2 of Major 6 Metropolitan cities and 40% if the Indian Railways. India on the other hand inherited a decrepit rail work.

B. the Method and origin of Partition

The Independence from British Empire prompted a wave of decolonization and spread across Asia and Africa. Yet alongside the Victories of Indias' Independence came the tragedies of Partition; whereby British ruled India divided into two separate and Independent States.

The violence that accompanied partition, which lead to the death of up to a million people and displacement of million were ranks among the worst holocaust of the twentieth century. Even after the lapse of 70 years world is still grappling with consequences of these seismic event in 1947. Not forever does the Bul Bul sing in balmy shades of bowers. Not forever lasts the spring. Nor ever blossom the flowers. Not forever reigneth Joy, set the sun on days of bliss, Friendship not for ever last they know not life who know this (Train to Pakistan- by Kushwanth singh)

The Pakistan: the Pakistan of India and Pakistan war perhaps of the most heart breaking event so history. Many and many lost. Its ripples are still felt every day in our culture, in our movies in our books. And for many of us in our personal lives as well. Let me bring you forth some shocking facts about the making of the two Countries which were always meant to stay together by saying Hindu Muslim Bhai-Bhai. The Rhyme of Iqbal who wrote that "Sare Jehan se Accha Hindustan Hamara. Hum Bul bule hai uske O gulsitan Hamara-Majahab nahi sikhatha aapas me bair karna" It is good and joyful country in the entire world – are its butterflies it is an enchanting garden shelter to Hindu land that was the aesthetic glory of Hindu India. No religion make you learn to fight amongst them". Such country is divided and torn out in to pieces and blood is still shedding it he crystal water of Ganga turning its water into red.

Although Independence was a product of decades of anti-colonial struggle, the more towards its final shape of action was dizzyingly swift. In fact 1947 British government announced its decision to withdraw from India. Political negotiations between British and Indian leaders followed with Jawaharlal Nehru representing the Indian National congress party and Mohammad Ali Jinnah serving as representative of Muslims League.

Whereas Jinnah called for national homeland for Muslim, whom he feared would be political disenfranchised the entire sub-continent. The British meanwhile were eager to disentangle

themselves from sub-continent politics and advanced the date of Independence to August 1947 a year sooner than Prime Ministers element Atlee promised. With the clock ticking in a radio address broad cast on June 3rd across British India, Nehru-Jinnah, Baldev singh representing the Sikh community and British Viceroy, Lord Mountbatten announced the plans for independence. These plans accept that a partition must occur and that it would divide the provinces of Bengal in the East and Punjab in the North west Cyril Radcliff was given a just six short week to determine India and Pakistan's new borders.

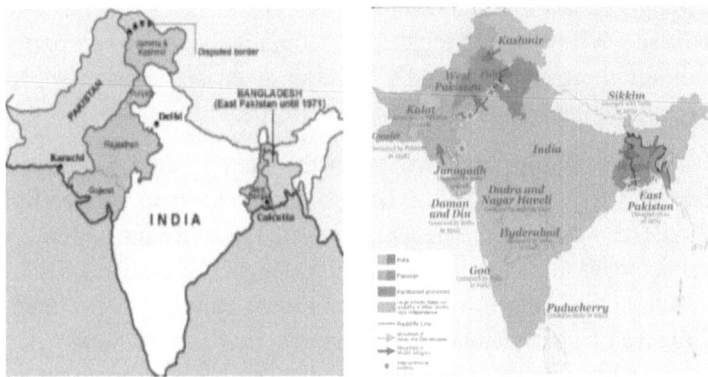

Final Map (Tentative Map proposed by Jinnah)

Nehru, Mohammad Ali Jinnah, Baldev Singh, and Dr. Ambedkar representing Hindu, Muslim Sikh and Scheduled Cast respectively, and the British Viceroy, Lord Mount Batten presided the conference of Partition, in the absence of Gandhi the plans of Partition which refers to that the Partition must occur and that would divide the Provinces of Bengal in the East and the Punjab in the North West, announced and addressed through Radio on June 3rd 1947 across the British India. The British Civil Servant assigned the monumental task of mapping this divide, Sir, Cyril Red Cliff was given six short week to determine the Indo-Pakistan's New Borders.

Redcliff's hastily drawn lines on the map created a political border where more had existed before. The map of Muslim Pakistan was secretly handed over to Lord Mount batten on earlier occasion, in which Punjab, Bengal, Hyderabad, Delhi and Jammu Kashmir where Muslims were heavily concentrated. Jinnah's original demand was whatever the land that was ruled by Muslim Moghuls prior to British should be taken in to the possession of Pakistan. Mountbatten argued that "before Moghuls, entire land was under the rule of Hindu Kings and

Emperors like Mouryans, Guptha and regional kingdoms like Vijayanagar in South, Rastra Kutakas Pandya's Sathavahanas in North and North West". Hence the proposal of Jinnah was rejected. He also said that "Your community (Muslim) were invaders and loot the booty and to expand your religion and hence they do not have right over any piece of land. Moreover Hindu majority is still prevailing in all parts of the India in spite of the forced conversions and which becomes their right to possess and protect their land. Further both Punjab, Sindh, Bengal both North and South are the lands where Hindu ancestor lived since three millennium. He further argued that "while acquiring any land either on sale or on gift, one has to see the mother document and on these lines also your claim will be null and void due that matter that your ancestors also were Hindus who lived in Hindu India since 4000 years back. Visit your Indian History you will get clarity. Isn't true?"

Mount Batten again said with serious voice that" we have convinced the Hindu leaders who were prepared to sacrifice their land to you foreigners in terms of religion. You better console yourself whatever the land they now are prepared to give is as a beneficiation of their mercy, mind it"

Jinnah could not argue further and felt satisfied whatever it is available is granted as approved. Thus the Areas with majority Muslim Population in the subcontinent's Northwest and North East became designated as Pakistan and Hindu majority area became India. This democratic logic believed as an the ground reality, in which Hindus and Muslims alongside Sikhs Christians and Others had lived side by side on all parts of Subcontinent. Yet with a toke of Cartographer's pen families and communities that virtually overnight, they had become religious "*Minorities* who now lived on *wrong* side of the new border. Way of this minority status, many people left their homes. Hindus and Sikhs fled into India; Muslims crossed in their other direction, into Pakistan. Around fifteen million religious refugees made this journey.

Most of the Intellectuals, Scholors and Historians offer many explanations why partition occurred. Some seek its underlying causes in the long history of colonialism which handicapped the population along religious lines, while for fostering the idea that Hindu and Muslims were distinct political communities. Many other see with critical eye on Indian Nationalism, which they argue was unable to overtake these divisions when imagining an Independent India. In spite of this others focus on the last decade colonial rule when the exigencies of the Second World War transformed the national political land scape reshaped motivations of provincial homeland. They also look towards the final political negotianism of 1947, which took place against a back drop of growing violence between religious communities that was fueled by propaganda that demonized "the other community and the fevered exhortations of political and local leaders.

Innocent common people bore the brunt of this violence. They were attacked and killed in their homes and neighborhoods and while travelling in convoys via train or on foot across the border. Women were raped assaulted and abducted in huge numbers as men made women's bodies the Warfield of communal identity. The populations of entire village were executed and corps lined the road sides. The violence was more of not exigency outcome but of preplanned and deliberately organized act.

The Punjab in particular was awash with weapons and recently de-mobilized soldiers who had fought in World War II. It was bluntly was an act of Muslim community who formed into paramilitary group who funded by local land owners and other elites who used chaos of partition to settled old scores, assert claims over land as it was their ancestral land to secure their own political and economic power.

The organized para military groups traversed the Punjab in campaigns of ethnic cleansing, these were few who could stop them. The British government forces for internal security, and consequently of British soldiers remained in their barracks on the villages, when the wrath of bloodshed is on.

C) Partition the division of British India in to the two separate states of India and Pakistan on 14th and 15th August 1947 was the last minute mechanism by which the British were able to secure agreement over how ***independence would take place***. At the time few people understood what partition would entail or what its results would be, and migration on enormous scale that followed took the vast majority contemporaries by surprise.

The main vehicle for nationalists' activity was the Indian National Congress whose best known leaders included Mahatma Gandhi, Jawaharlal Nehru. Even before the 1940 it had long argued for a unitary state with strong Center; even though Congress was ostensibly secular in its objectives, organization representing minority interests increasingly viewed this idea with suspicion believed that it would entrench the political dominance of Hindus what made up about 80% of the population. At around 25% of its population, Muslims were British India's largest religious minority. Under Imperial rule they had grown accustomed to having their minority status protected by a system of political control hinged on identifications of interest groups willing to collaborate a governing style described as "divide and Rule"

The prospect of losing this protection on independence drew closer worried more and more Muslims first in parts of Northern India and then after World War II in the influential Muslim-Majority provinces of Bengal and Punjab.

(D)Torn Apart: Partition triggered riots, mass causalities and colossal wave of migration. Millions people moved to what they *hoped would be safer territory*, with Muslim heading towards Pakistan and Hindus Sikh in the direction India. As many as 14-15 million people may have been eventually displaced, travelling on front in bullock, carts, by foot or by train. Above are the images taken by a European Photographer which speaks by themselves about the irony that *Indian Hindus were cruelly treated in their own ancestral land? Muslims and Europeans came here to India both for their selfish motive of Spice trade and expansion of their monotheistic violent religions which were imposed upon the Hindus' heads by sword and violence and finally took wrathful decision to occupy land of the Hindu India and titled it as Pakistan. It is not a Pakistan (clean and holy space) but it is Khoonitan as the blood of Hindus flown like river in that area. They made dirt of Indian Ganga through the rivers of blood studded by Hindu population* Estimated deaths of death toll partition ranges from 200,000 to two million. Many were killed during the transition; by members of other communities and same times their own families as well as by contagious diseases which swept through refugee camp. Women often swept through refugee camps. Women often targeted as symbols of community honor, with up to 100,000 raped and abducted.

What can explain the intensely violent reaction? Many of the people concerned were very deeply attached not just too religious identity but to territory, and Britain was reluctant to use its troops to maintain law and order. The situation was especially dangerous in Punjab, where weapons and demolished soldiers were abundant.

Another unforeseen consequence of partition was that Pakistan's population ended up mostly homogenous than originally anticipated. The Muslim League's leaders and assumed that Pakistan, non-Muslims minorities comprised only 1.61% of Population by 1951, compared with 22% east Pakistan (now in Bangladesh)

And even though Pakistan was an ostensibly created as a "homeland" for Indias' Muslim minority, not all Muslim even supported its formation, never mind migrated there. Muslims remained the largest minority group in an Independent India, making up around 10% of the population in 1951. Gandhi himself was assassinated in January 1948 by a Hindu nationalist extremist who blamed for being too supportive to Muslims at the time of partition.

He organized Sathyagraha moment for granting minimum 50 million rupees for the Muslim Pakistan as an emergency grant to combat the economic delusion? That is the ideology of our Indian Hindu who always at the service humanity since their Namaste connotes that "*the divine in me bows the divine in you*" that is the respect with humility is given by a Hindu irrespective of other being a Hindu or a Muslim or any other caste. It is enough if he is a human." Even the British failed to show their humanity which boast that it is Jesus Christ that dictated them to be Christian and a Christian is who condole the sins of another being irrespective a believer or non-believer.

Readers must be known of the facts how they behaved with Indian. Even the Premier of English Crown Mr. Churchill has passed remarks that " Hindu's are *rustic and savage people much lower than dogs and animals*" Such is the view of high statured Prime Minister of British Empire where Sun doesn't set**" For his information (of course he is no more now) he and his** European people had borrowed the Science, numerology, Surgery, decimal system, geometry, astrology and Algebra from Indian saints who theorized and practiced in from Hindus' day to day life around5000 BC back.

Both states subsequently faced huge problems accommodating and rehabilitant post-partition refugees, whose numbers swelled when the Two States went to war the disputed territory of Jammu and Kashmir in 1947-48. Later bouts communal people still migrating on late as the 1960. Today two countries relationship is far from healthy Kashmir remains a flash point; both countries are nuclear armed Indian Muslims are frequently suspected of harboring loyalties toward Pakistan. Non-Muslim minorities in Pakistan are increasingly vulnerable thanks to the so called Islamisation of life there since the 1980's. Seven decades as well over a billion people still live in the shadow of Partition.

Section B
Indian Annexation of Hyderabad Deccan

Hyderabad State was initially a"Subah" (Regional sub-ordinate Kingdom) in the Moghul Empire, inn Deccan plateau. Nizam ul Mulk Asaf Jah was appointed as "Subahdar" in 1713 my Mughal Empire. Hyderabad's effective Independence is dated to 1724, when the Nizam won Military victory over rival military Appointee.

In 1798 Hyderabad became the first Indian Royal State to accede to British Protection under the Policy of subsidiary alliance instituted by Arthur Wellesley. The state of Nawab under the leadership of its 7th Nizam Mir Usman Ali was the largest and most prosperous of all princely states in India with an annual revenue of over 9crores. It covered 82,698 square Miles (214 190 K) of fairly homogenous territory and comprised a population of roughly was 16.34 million people as per 1941 census) of which a majority (85%) was Hindu. The stated had its own Army, airline, telecommunication system, Railway Network Postal system, and Currency and Radio Broadcasting service. It was like a separate country within our country India.

Hyderabad was multilingual state consisting of Peoples speaking Telugu (48.2%) Marathi (26.4 %) Kannada (12.3) and Urdu 10.3%) In spite of the overwhelming Hindu Majority, Hindus were severely underrepresented in government, Police, Military Services. Of 1765 Officers in the State Army, 1268 were Muslims 521 Hindus and 121 others were Christian, Parsis and Sikhs. Of the officials drawing salary of Rs. 600-1200 Per month 59 were Muslims 5 were Hindus and 38 were of other religions. The Nizam and his nobles who were mostly Muslims owned 40% of the total land in the State.

When the British departed from Indian sub-continent in 1947 they offered the various principle states in the cob-continent the option of acceding to either India or Pakistan or staying as an Independent State. Several large States including Hyderabad declined to join either inn India or Pakistan. Hyderabad had been part of the calculations of all India Political parties since 1930's

The leaders of the New Union of India were wary of Balkanization of India if Hyderabad was left Independent . Hyderabad state had been steadily becoming more theocratic since the beginning of the 20th century. In 1926, Mahmud Nawaz Khan a retired Hyderabad official founded the Majlis-e-Ittehad Musclemen also known as Ittehad of MIM). *"Its objective were to unite the Muslims in the State in support of Nizam and reduce the Hindu majority by large-scale conversion to Islam."*

The MIM became a powerful communal Organization with the principled focus to marginalize the political aspirations of Hindus and Moderate Muslims.

Operation Polo: the code of the Hyderabad "Police action was a military operation in September 1948 in which the Indian Armed forces invaded the State of Hyderabad , annexing the State into the Independent Indian Union.

At the time of Partition in 1947 the Princely states of India who in Principle had self-governments within their own territories were subject to *subsidiary* alliance with British giving them the control of their external relations. In Indian Independence Act 1947, the British abandoned all such alliances leaving the states with option of opting for full Independence. However by 1948 almost all had *acceded* to either India or Pakistan. One Major exception was that of the Wealthiest and Most powerful principality, Hyderabad where the Nizam Usman Ali Asif Zahi VII, a Muslim Sunni Ruler who presided over a largely Hindu Population chose Independence and hoped to maintain this with an irregular army recruited from Muslim atrocity known **as Razakars**.

The Nizam was also beset by Telangana Uprising, which was unable to subjugate.

The Indian government was anxious to avoid it what iternal independence within India, termed as Balkanization of what had been the Indian Empire determined to the effect the integration of Hyderabad in to the new Indian amidst atrocities by the Razakars the Indian Home Minister Sardar Patel

decided to annex Hyderabad in what term Police action. The operation itself took five days in which the Razakars and Hyderabad militancy was defeated swiftly. The operation lead massive violence on communal lines the Indian Minister Jawaharlal Lal Nehru appointed commission known as the Sunderlal committee. Its report which not released until 2013 concluded that as a conservative estimates 27,000 to 40,000 people had lost their lives during and after the police action. Other Scholors have put the figure at 200,000.

CHAPTER 10

INDO PAKISTAN RELATION AFTER PARTITION

Key Events in India and Pakistan relations: A time line of August 1947 –Britain ends its colonial rule over the Indian Subcontinent, which becomes two independent nations, Hindu majority but secularly governed India and the Islamic Republic of Pakistan. The division widely known as Partition, sparks massive rioting that kills up to one million while another 15 million people flee their homes in one of the world's worst tragedy of human migration. A camp displaced Indian Muslims next to Humayuns tomb in New Delhi during the period of unrest following the partition of India and Pakistan.

1947-48: The first Indo Pakistan war over Kashmir is fought after armed tribes men (Lashker Toeba LeT) from Pakistan's North West frontier Province now called Khyber Pakhunkhawa invaded the dispute Territory in October **1947.** The Maharaja, forced with an internal revolt as well as external invasion request the assistance of the Indian armed forces in return for acceding to India. He hands over control of his defense communications and foreign affairs to the Indian government.

Both side agree that instrument of accession signed by Maharaja Hari Sing be ratified a referendum to beheld after hostilities have ceased. Historians on either side of the dispute remain undecided as to whether the Maharaja signed the document after India troops had enter Kashmir (that is under duress or if under no direct military pressure.)

Fighting continues through second half of 1948, with regular Pakistan Army called upon to protect Pakistan borders.

The war officially ends on January 1, 1949 when United Nations arranges a ceasefire, with an established ceasefire, a UN Peace Keeping force and recommendation that the referendum on the accession of the Kashmir to India to held as argued earlier. That referendum has yet to be held.

The Indian (Eastern) side of the cease fire line is referred to as Jammu and Kashmir. Both countries refer to the other side of the cease fire line as "occupied territory" 1954. The accession of Jammu and Kashmir to India ratified by the States' constituent assembly.

1957: The Jammu and Kashmir constituent assembly approves a constitution. India, from the point of the 1954 ratification and 1957 constitution, begins to refer to Jammu and Kashmir an integral part of the Indian Union.

1963: Following the 1962 (Hindu China Bhai Bhai) Sino-Indian war, the foreign ministers of India and Pakistan Swaran Singh and Zulfiquar Ali Bhutto holds talks under auspicious of the British and American regarding the Kashmir dispute. The specific contents of these talks have not yet been declassified, but no agreement was reached. In the talks "Pakistan signified willingness to consider approaches other than a plebiscite and India recognized that the status of Kashmir was in dispute and territorial adjustments might be necessary "according to a declassified U. S Statement Memo dated 27 January 1964.

1964: Following the failure of the 1963 talks, Pakistan refers the Kashmir case to the U.N. Security Council

1965: India and Pak fight their second war. The conflict begins after a clash between border patrols in April in the Rann of Kutch (in the Indian state of (Gujarat) but escalates on August 5, when between 26000 and 33000 Pakistani soldiers cross the ceasefire line dressed as Kashmir locals crossing into Indian administered Kashmir. Infantry armor and air force units are involved in the conflict while it remains localized to the Kashmir theatre, but as the war expands Indian troops cross the Indian National Border at Lahore on September 6. The largest engagement of the war taken place in the Sialkot section where between 400 and 600 tanks square off in an inconclusive battle. By September 2 both sides agree to a UN mandated cease fire ending the war that had by that point reached stalemate, with both sides holding of the other's terrorism.

1966: On January 10, 1966, India Prime Minister Lal Bahadur Sastry and Pakistan President Ayub Khan sign agreement at Tashkent (Now Uzbekistan) agreeing to withdraw to pre August lines that Economic and diplomatic relation would be restored.

1971: India and Pakistan to war a third time and this war was on the liberation of East Pakistan to liberate from West Pakistan dominance and this war was for the third over. The conflict begins when the central Pakistan to subside the issue of Kashmir. The conflict begins when the central Pakistani government in West Pakistan led by Zulfiquar Ali Bhutto refuses to allow Awami League on Dhaka that begins in March, but India becomes involved in the conflict in December, after

the Pakistani Air Force launches a pre-emptive strike on air field in India's North West. India then launches a coordinated land, air and Sea assault on East Pakistan. The Pakistan army surrendered at Dhaka, and its army of more than 90,000 become prisoners of War. Hostilities lasted 13 days making this one of the shortest wars in Modern history. East Pakistan became Independent country of Bangladesh on December 6, 1971.

1972: Pakistan Prime Minister Zulfiquar Ali Bhutto and Indian Prime Minister India Gandhi sign an agreement in the Indian town of Shimla, in which both countries agree to "Put an end to the conflict and confrontation that have hither to marred their relations and work for the promotion of a friendly and harmonious relationship and the establishment of a durable peace in the Sub-continent." Both sides agree to settle any disputes" by peace terms.

The Shimla agreement designate the ceasefire line of ***December Line 17, 1971***, as being the new "***Line of control(LoC)*** between the two countries, which neither side is to seek to alter unilaterally and which "shall be respected by both sides without prejudice to the recognized position of either side.

1974: Kashmir Government affirmed that the State "is a constituent of the Union of India. In May, India exploded a nuclear device at Pokhram referred by India as a peaceful nuclear device explosive." The operation was code named "smiling Buddha

1988: The two countries signed an agreement which was later ratified, that neither side will attack the others nuclear installations of faculties which include "nuclear power and research reactors, fuel fabrication, Uranium enrichment, isotopes separation and reprocessing facilities as well as any other installation with fresh or irradiated nuclear fuel and materials in any form and establishments storing significant quantities of radioactive material.

They also agreed to share the latitude and longitudes and all nuclear installations and have been sharing and formed militant wings which displayed armed resistance to the Indian-rule in the valley.

Pakistan said that it gave its "Moral and diplomatic support to the movement and called for the earlier UN sponsored referendum again. In blamed Pakistan for providing weapons and training to the fighters and called as "cross border Terrorism." The allegation was refuted by Pakistan. The armed resistance continued through the 1990s and was also fueled in part by and large influx of Mujahedeen who took Part in the Afghan war against the Soviet in 1980's

1991 Agreement: A. B. Vajpayee, Prime Minister of India rides a bus to the Pakistan at Lahore to meet Pakistan counterpart Nawaz sheriff and signed a major peace accord.

1999 May- Conflict erupt in Kargil as Pakistani forces and occupy Himalayan Peaks launches air and grounded strikes. General Pervez Musharraf, the Pakistan Chief of army leas military coup deposing Nawaz sheriff, the then Prime Minister and installing himself as the head of the government.

2002 October- The stands of ends.

2004 January: Musharraf and Vajpayee hold talks launching a bilateral negotiations to settle outstanding issues.

2007 February: Samjhoutha Express Train is bombed India and Pakistan Northern India killing 68.

2008 October: India and Pakistan trade routes across Kashmir for the first time in Six decades.

2008 November: Gunman attack Mumbai killing 166 people. The gunmen arrived through sea rout. India blame Pakistan based Terror group Lashkar-e-Toeba. Mumbai Taj Mahal palace Hotel on fire after terror Attack.

2014 May: India New Prime Minister Namenda Modi invites Pakistan counterpart Nawaz Sheriff to New Delhi for his inauguration.

2015 December2:15 pm: Indian Prime Minister Narender Modi makes a surprise visit to Pakistan city of Lahore on birthday and wedding of his granddaughter.

2016 January 2: Six gunmen attack on Indian Air force in Northern town of Pathankot, killing seven soldiers in battle that lasted nearly four days.

2016 July: Indian soldiers kill Kashmir terrorist and Hizbul Mujahedeen leader Burhan Warsi sparking mouth of anti-India protests and deadly clashes in the region.

2016 September: Suspected Terrorists sneak into Indian Army base in Kashmir URI and kill 18 soldiers. Four attackers are also killed 11 days later Indian Army said to have carried out surgical strikes to destroy terror launch pads across the line of border.

CHAPTER 11

OPEN FOR OPENION

Hypotheses cannot be forged to fact unless it is applied to Experiment.

The arrival of Muslim invaders a thousand years ago dramatically transformed the Hindu culture. Like in any invasion, these war destructions mayhem and trauma. Hindu in Afghanistan literally means "kills of Hindu slaves during early phase of this invasion and ruins of Vijayanagar by confederacy of Muslim kings are testimony to later phase.

However, the damage was neither absolute nor permanent over time the ever resilient Hindu culture recovered and adapted itself to the new realities and eventually a new Hindu a culture emerged that engaged with Islam both philosophically and socially.

The Indian sub-continent is relatively isolated from the rest of the world because of the Himalayas bordering the north and the sea bordering the South. Still people have come through mountain passes and sea ports for over five thousand year. Some came to rule, some came for the purpose of Spice trade, some came to loot, some came to rule, some came to convert idolaters to infinite ideology of Monotheism and some came for a better home. Each one who came to India with a desire to change to their own faith to be imposed upon Indian Hindu, like Islam or Communist idealism? But India remained unchanged so strong like Himalayan height not to embrace to their ideology. They bore their torture, plunder, rape and loot but they stacked firm in their faith. Most of the women felt it hurt and got self-immolation instead of yielding to their order. Men became either slave or death as a penalty but never surrender themselves. That strong will made them to maintain their heritage intact even in modern days. Though they were stubborn in the matter of religion but remain influenced to foreign invaders over its history in various degrees: from Egyptians, Persian Arabs Chinese, Greek, roman Central Asians and finally Europeans.

Indian culture is like a Pop box (Masala Box). The dominant spices we identify as Hindu but not all them came to being here following indigenous challenges as the rise of Buddhism, which introduced ideas of Monastic orders. Others cane to being following foreign challenges such as arrival of the Greek who introduced the idea of stone temples enshrining stone images of heroes and gods, very different and Mountain tree gods of local tribes. Some spices refuse to be identified as Hindu but do not mind being called Indian. Some spices insists identified as non-Indian. Then these are spices that are best called global as they found everywhere on the earth. Indian Hindus though they tough in getting converting their faith save some neglected caste; but culturally they are too tolerate and accommodate and get adjusted with any culture that encountered. Some invaders left them to their fate some killed and this is the fate.

There are many Indians and Hindus who believe in the idea of "Pure" culture. Notions of "Purity" are always mythological (subjective), never scientific (objective) however they play a key role in shaping culture. This becomes evident when one thinks about the influence of the Portuguese on India. Portuguese brought Potato to India from South America; they also spread Christianity. Many Purists don't see Potato as a foreign vegetable. But they see Christian as a foreign idea, but hate it vehemently, even as they eat alooparatha (Aloo bread).

Islam rose 1400 year ago. Islam reached Kerala via Sea route for spice business during the life time of the Prophet Muhammad. When we usually refer to Invasion of North India (Punjab and Gangetic plains) that eventually impacted the East (Bengal) and then the rest of the sub-continent. This happened in two phase first less successful one spear headed by Arabs that reached the borders of India nearly 1200 years ago and the second more successful one spear headed by Turks and Moghul that began 800 years.

When the matter of religion comes, Historians avoid the term Islamic invasions "and prefer using the worlds like Arab, Turk and Mongol or Moghul invasions because to two reasons. Firstly, many see these invasions were motivated by economics and Politics not religion. Secondly that they want avoid the communal vocabulary. Many Hindus feel the very same historians do not give Hinduism in the same respect. It is why because they argue that "if you do not think Islam to violence, how can you ling Hinduism to casteism. Why cannot both nor religion? "

In the early invasions most of India remained unaffected. The spread of Islam destroyed the Buddhist and Zoroastrian centers thrive along Silk Road and Incense route. This would have sent shockwaves across the world. If these was any impact on Indian thought, it was indirect not direct. Some people say that although Bhakti and monotheism is alluded in the 2000 years old Bhagavad-Gita, the wide spread popularity of Bhakti and Monotheistic ideas in the last 1000 years may have been the result of Islamic influence. The phase two of Islamic invitation saw great violence. Warlords from Afghanistan and Central Asia such as

Gaznavides sought to loot the legendary weal of India, mostly hoarded in temples. Fuel for their raids was provided by both trades and religious zeal to wipeout the land of Idolaters. These invaders wiped cities and temple in their wake and went back with old and new slaves. Spice trade turned into slave trade.

We can argue endlessly on how much damage physical and how much psychological how much was real how much was propaganda, how much was motivated by economics and how much religious zeal. But the fact is Hinduism was never the same. It is flexible and cushion attached democratic one as for as tolerance point of view. Hindu sentiments are almost dharma and Karmic

one who consoles by themselves that whatever had happened is Karma related result and it must be the fruits of previous birth's Karma. They never have attributed either good or bad happening on account of political exaggeration.

Those who came to Hindu India like warlords of Afghans and Moghuls instantaneously decided to settle India seeing on observing the greatness of their tolerance and natures' rich resources in Indian subcontinent. From around 800 years a sultanate rose to Delhi led my Mamulks, Khiljis, Lodhis, Tughlaq and Deccan regimes. From around 400 years ago the Mughal Empire established itself in North India which gradually spread to the South.

Temples such Madurai in the South, Ujjain in Central India, Puri in the east Somnath in the West retained memory of plunder by Muslim Kings in local lore. But in these times, dramatic changes took place in Hinduism. Some happened because of Islam others despite it. While many temples such as Kashmir, Gujarat and Gangetic plains were destroyed, their pillars were used to build Mosques, many new grand temples were built on ancient sites by local Hindu kings in the last thousand years to show their strength of power. Current edifices Jagannath Temple that we see today that we see today was built in 800nyears ago by Chandagangadeva. Again most of the grand structures we see in Tamil Nadu and Andhra Pradesh such as Meenakshi Temple in Madurai are about 400 years old, built by Nayak kings. In the North People avoided building temples and choose to worship the deity inside homes, giving rise to the Thakur-ghar or Haroli culture seen in Rajasthan.

Further it is within 1000 years that Acharya's such as Sankaracharya, Ramanujacharya Madhvacharya Vallabha, Nimbaska and Chaitanya consolidated theistic Vedanta Philosophy that today seen by many as main revised foundations of Hinduism. It is also within the last thousand years we find the rise of various sacred Hindu literature in regional languages including almost of the Ramayana and Mahabharata that we

find in Tamil, Telugu, Malayalam, Kannada, Assamese, Odia, Bengali, Gujarati, Marathi, Marwari, and Hindi.

Bhakti songs of Meera, Ravidas, Tukaram, Annam Acharya, Khestreyya and Purandara Dasa were all written in the past 500 years. While oral traditions has been the main stay of Hinduism, in many Hindu communities manuscripts of the Bhagawad Gita of the or the Ramayana started being enshrined worshipped, for example Bhagavad Gita-ghara in Oriya, indicating the increasingly popular value given to the book, clearly was an Islamic influence.

In the past 400 years Sultan's Deccan Patronized Hindustani classical music, Nawab's of Oudh Celebrated Krishna leela and

Ramaleela, established the Bade Mangal Festival of Hanuman in Lucknow, Holi became a royal festival celebrated by Hindu Muslim Kings. The Moghul court patronized Persian painters who established the Indian miniature style of painting that resulted in fine art works for various local Rajput kings and Hindu Noblemen as themes from the Ramayana, Mahabharata, GithaGovinda, Bhagavad Gita and the puranas. There are displayed in museum around the world.

Rural areas were organized along caste lines before arrival of Islam and the system is continued even after the arrival of Islam. Those who converted to Islam or Christianity continued to follow that family vocations while retaining their caste.

There were many communities where the lines between Hinduism and Islam were not rigid. For example, many Rajasthan musicians who sang Hindu songs bardielore were Muslim. In Bengal *patuapainters* who painted the epics on long pieces of Paper were Muslims. In Kerala there is the Mapilla Ramayana of the Malabar Muslims where we find words like Sharia, used in Ramayana. The famous Ballard Padmavath about the attack on chitor by Allauddin Khilji was compose by a Muslim poet Malik Muhammad Jayasi. In many shrines, holy men were seen as *pirs* by Muslim and as Jogis by Hindus. Many Muslim kings had Hindu courtiers (Man Singh in Tansen in the court of Akbar) and many Hindu kings had Muslim courtiers (Hakim Khan Sur who fought alongside Rana Pratap in Haldhighat)

Now customs changed, in North India, the Ghunghat or covering of women's head and faces became common in Hindu Households, a practice still not seen in south. In Temples of Shrinathji in Nathdwara one of the many attires of the deity was Moghul-Vesha. (Moghul Dress). In many parts of the south, the dieties had Muslims guards and Muslim companions such as Vavar of Ayyappa-Swami and Muttahala Revuttam of Draupadi Amman.

According to one theory, Islam acquired a unique Indian flavor. Only here di Islam co-exist with another religion in harmony. In Europe, it fought bitter religious wars in Christianity. In South

East Asia, Buddhism and Hinduism were seen as foundational culture influences, but with Islam clearly as the religion on Top. In India, Islam became the practice in certain Castes. For Example there could be *"high Caste"* land owners who were also Muslim or there were "*Low Caste*" butchers who also happened to be Muslims. This created a kind of tension filled hormone with violence on the edges, but no full-fledged communal conflict.

It was British who preferred o see as a collection of religious rather than collection of castes. They defined Hinduism and make it a collection of castes, excluding the caste status of those who followed Abrahamic Religions, village reality notwithstanding. It was the British who tried to face-fit 3000 *Jatis* of India into four *varnas* of the Vedas. Caste politics meant no *Jathi* had majority anywhere in India and was too complicated to handle. Religion politics meant Indians could very easily be distracted by communal politics.

Independent India tried to suppress (export) caste and religious politics, but could not escape language politics. Now we are faced with caste, religious and language politics that often distract us from the economic woes of the land. Even if there was no Islam, Indians would still have to face the issue of Caste and language and even gender politics.

History, politics, Economics, culture and Religion are very complex subjects. When people try to simply Indian history by speaking of 1000 years of Muslim enslavement of Hindus (or that Brahmins Enslaved dalits or Sanskrit is source all wisdom) we need to be vigilant about the manipulative nature of these *half-truths*. Incomplete truths are often more dangerous that falsehoods. Invasions like drought and epidemics, result in migration and shifts in population and recalibration of culture. There is a transplantation and transformation of ideas. And so Americans today practice Yoga not realizing its Indian (or should we say Hindu) roots; Indians drink coffee not realizing its Arabic (or should we say Muslims) roots.

CHAPTER 12

HINDUS IN PAKISTAN AND MUSLIMS IN INDIA -A SKETCH

(A) HINDUISM IN PAKISTAN AFTER PARTITION OF INDIA:

The population of Hindu comprise approximately 1.85% of Pakistan Population. According to the 1998 census Hindu population was 20% in 1947 in Pakistan at the time of Division. As of 2010 Pakistan had the fifth largest Hindu Population in the world and PEW predicts that by 2050 Pakistani will have fourth largest Population in the world. Further, as per the Research Report of PEW the Hindu population will reach 5.6 million and Hindus will constitute 2% Pak Population by 2050.

Pakistan gained Independence from British India on 14th August 1947, 4.7 million of West Pakistan's Hindus and Sikhs migrated to India while 6.5 million moved from India to live in West Pakistan. The 1998 Census the Hind Population was found to be 2,443,614. Hindus are found in all provinces of Pakistan but are mostly concentrated in Sindh. They speak variety of languages such as *Sindh, Seraiki, Aer, Dhatki Gera, Gurgula, Jaandara, Kabutra, Koli, Larki, Saans, Vaghri and Gujarati*.

Rig-Veda the oldest text was believed to have been composed in the Punjab region of Modern-day Pak (former India) on the banks of river Indus around 1500 BCE. The Sindh Kingdom and its rulers play an important role in the Indian Epic story of Mahabharata. In addition, a Hindu legend States that the Pakistani city of Lahore was first founded Lava while Kasur was found by his twin brother Kusha, both of whom were the sons of Rama of the Ramayana. The legendary kingdom Gandhara people are also a major part of Hindu literature such as Ramayana, and Mahabharata. Many Pakistani names such as Peshawar and Multan can be traced back to Sanskrit roots.

In accordance with the Census of 1998 of Pakistan separate caste Hindu constitutes about 1.6% of the total population Pakistan and about 6.6% in the Sindh Province. The Pak census separate scheduled caste from main body of Hindus who make a further 0.25% of National Population Based on 1998 census as well as stabilization of Pakistan's Hindu Population since then Pakistan would today have roughly 3 million Hindus. According to Election Commissioner of Pakistan there are 1.49 million Hindu voters in the country who are mostly concentrated in Sindh.

Decline: There has been historical decline of Hinduism, Buddhism and Sikhism in the area of Pakistan. This happened for a variety of reasons even as here religions have continued to flourish beyond the Eastern frontiers of Pakistan. The region became predominantly Muslim during Rule of Delhi sultanate and late Moghul Empire. In general religion conversions was a gradual process with many *converting to Islam to gain tax relief, land grant, marriage Partner social and economic advancement or freedom from slavery.* The Predominantly Muslim population supported Muslim League and Pakistan Movement.

Some Hindus in Pakistan feel that they *are treated as second class citizens and many have continued to migrate to India.* According to the Human rights commission of Pakistan data, just around 1000 families fled to India in 2013. In 2014 many members of the ruling Pakistan Muslim League Nawaz (PML-N) Dr. Ramesh Kumar Vankwani revealed in the National Assembly of Pakistan around 5000 Hindus are migrating from Pakistan to India every Year.

At the time of formation of Hindu land of West as Pakistan, the hostage theory had been espoused. According to the theory the Hindu Minority in Pakistan was to be given affair deal in Pakistan in order to ensure the protection of the Muslim minority in India. However Khwaja Nazimuddin the 2nd Prime Minister of Pakistan stated "I do not agree that religion is a private affair of the individual nor do I agree that in an Islamic state every citizen has identical rights, no matter what his caste, creed or faith be"

After Independence in 1947 over 4.7 million Hindus and Sikh from west Pakistan left to India and 6.5 million close to migrate to Pakistan. The reasons for this exodus were heavily communal atmosphere in the British Raj deep distrust of each other, the brutality of violent mobs and the antagonism between religious communities. That over a million people lost their lives in the bloody violence of 1947, should attest to the fear and hate that filled the hearts of millions of Hindus Muslim Sikh who left ancestral homes hastily after Independence

Dr. Ramesh Kumar Vankwani revealed in the National Assembly of Pakistan that 5000 Hindus are migrating from Pakistan to India every year. These Pakistani Hindus who have migrated top India allege that Hindu girls are sexually harassed in Pakistani Schools adding that Hindu students are made to read the Quran and their religious practices are mocked. The Indian government is planning to issue Aadhaar cards and Pan cards to Pakistani Hindu Refugees and simplifying the process by which they can acquire Indian citizenship.

In the after math of the Babri Masjid demolition widespread retaliatory riots erupted against Hindus Mobs attacked scores of Hindu temples in Sukkur, Sindh homes and temples also attacked in Quetta. In 2005 around 52 Hindus were killed by firing near Nawab Akbar Bugtis residences during bloody clashes between Bugti tribes' men and para military forces in Baluchistan.

At the time of Pakistan the hostage theory had been expounded. According to this theory the Hindu Minority in Pakistan was to be given a fair deal in Pakistan in order to ensure the protection of the Muslim minority in India. However Khwaja Nazimuddin the 2nd Prime Minister of Pakistan stated "I do not agree that religion is a private affair of the Individual nor do agree that in an Islamic state every citizen has identical rights no matter what his cast creed or faith be"

The raise of Taliban insurgency in Pakistan have been an influential and increasing factor in the persecution and discrimination against religious minorities particularly Indu and Sikhs. In July 2010 around 60 members of the minority Hindu community in Karachi were attacked and evicted from their homes following incident of a ***Dalit Hindu youth drinking water from a tap near an Islamic Mosque.*** In January 2014 a Police man standing guard outside a Hindu temple at Peshawar was gunned down.

Pakistan Curriculum Issue: According to sustainable development Policy Institute report "Associated with the influence on the ideology of Pakistan has been an essential component of hate against India and the Hindus. For the upholders of ideology of Pakistan the existence of Pakistan is defined only in relation to Indus and hence Hindus have to be pained as negatively as possible. A 2005 reportedly the National commission for Justice and Peace, a nonprofit organization in Pakistan found that Pakistan Study of Text books in Pakistan have been used to articulate the hatred that Pakistan policy makers have attempted to inculcate towards Hindu. "Vituperative animosities legitimize military and arctucrati rule nurturing a siege mentality. Pakistan studies Text Books are an active site to represent India as a "***hostile neighbor***" the report stated. The Story of Pakistan's past is intentionally written to be distinct from and often in direct contracts with, interpretations of history found in India. From the Government issued students Text books students are taught that Hindus are backward and superstitious. Further report stated "Text Books" reflect international obfuscation.

(B) Muslims and other Minority In India:

Islam is the second largest religion in India with 24.2% of the country's population or roughly 172 million people identify as adherents of Islam (as per 2011 census)

Spice trade Relations have existed between Arabia and Indian Sub-continent since ancient times. But newly Islamized Arab were Islam's first contact with India. Historians Eliot and Dowson say in their book "The History of India, as told by its own Historians" that the first ship bearing a Muslim travelers was seen on the Indian Coast as early as 6300 CE. H.G.Rawlinson in his book "Ancient and Medieval History of India" claims that the Arab Muslims settled on the Indian coast in the last part of 7th Century (Zain Uddin Mukhdoom-Tuhafat-ul-Mujahedeen" is also a reliable work. This fact is corroborated by J. Sturrock in his Madras District Manuals and by Haridas Bhattacharya in his Book "Cultural Heritage of India Volume IV". It was with advent of Islam that the Arabs became prominent cultural Force in the world. ***Arab Countries and Spice Traders became carriers of the new Religion and they propagated it wherever they went*** (a sort of peaceful missionary work). T

The first Indian, Cheraman Juma Mosque is thought to have been built inn 629 CE in Kerala by Malik Deena although same historians say the first Mosque was inn Gujarat. In Malabar Mappilas may have been the first community to convert to Islam. Intensive missionary activities were carried out along the Coast and many other natives embraced Islam. Thus among Mappilas we find both the descendants of Arab through local women and converts from among the local people.

In 8th Century Mohammad bib Qasim conquered the prince of Sindh. Sindh became the ***Eastern most province of the Umayyad Caliphate*** about we have come across in the earlier sections for the rest of history up to Partition.

When the partition was set forth the Indian Independence Act 1947 and resulted in the dissolution of the British Indian Empire and the end of British Raj. It resulted in a struggle between the newly constituted states of India and Pakistan and displaced up to 125 million with estimates of loss of life varying from several hundred thousand to a million (the most estimated figure is 10 to 12 million) crossed the boundaries between India and Pakistan in 1947. The violent nature of the A Partition created an atmosphere of mutual hostility and suspicious between India and Pakistan that plague their relationship to the day.

After partition of India in 1947, two thirds of the Muslim resided in Pakistan (both east and West Pakistan) but a third resided in India. Based on 1951 Census persons 7,226,000 Muslims went to Pak (both to the East and West) from India while 7,249,000 Hindu Sikhs moved to the India from Pakistan. Some critics allege that the British hast inn the Partition process increased violence that followed.

However many argue that the British were forced to expedite the partition by events on the ground. Once in Office Mountbatten quickly became aware if Britain were to avoid involvement of civil War which seemed increasingly likely there was no alternative to partition and a hasty exit from India. Law and order broken down many before partition with much bloodshed on both sides. A massive Civil war looking by the time Mountbatten became Viceroy. After the Second world War Britain had limited resources and perhaps insufficient to the task of keeping the Military power to enforce law and order. Historian Lawrence James concurs that in 1947 Mountbatten was left with no option to act and run.

The conflicts between Hinduism and Muslims in Indian sub-continent has a complex history which can be said to have begun with Umayyad caliphate's invasion of Sindh in 711. The presentation of Hindus during the Islamic expansion in India in the medieval period was characterized by destruction of temples like Somanatha and the anti-Hindu practice of the Moghul Emperor Aurangzeb which was fresh in the memories of Hindus. Although there are many instances of conflict between two groups; number of Hindus worshipped and continue to worship the tombs of Muslim Sufi saint's leadership and organization.

- The Ajmer Sharif Darga and Darga of Ala Hazrath at Bareilly sheriff are prime centers of Sufi oriented Sunni Muslim India.
- Indian Shia Muslims forms substantial within the Muslim community of India comprising between 25-31% of total Muslim Population in an estimation alone during 2005-

06 of the then Indian Muslim Population of 157 million. Source like the Indian and DNA reported that India's Shia Population during that a period; around 40,000,000 to 50,000,000 of the total 157,000,000 Indian Muslim Population.

- The Deobandi Movement, another section of the Sunni Muslim population originate from the Darul-ul-loom Deoban, an influential religious seminary in the district of Saharanpur of Uttar Pradesh. The Jaitul-Ulema-e-Hind founded by Deoban scholars in 19919 became a political Mouth piece of Dar-ul-uloom.

- The Jamat-e-Islami Hind founded in 1941, advocates the establishment of an Islamic government and has been active in promotion of Education, social service and ecumenical outreach to the community.

- There are around notable Islamic Scholors and activists who supported the stay in India itself instead of leaving to unknown place.

- Government of India introduced the subsidized the cost of airfare for Hajj Pilgrimage though Hajj subsidy is technical violation of sharia, since the Quran declares that Hajj should be performed by Muslims using their own resources.

- Muslim Personal Law is introduced and included in the provisions of the Constitution so as to enjoy the residing Muslims as a protection for living in India. Thus personal laws cannot be challenged as being violates part III of the Constitution of India, though it violate of the Constitutional provision of Article 44 which envisages a uniform civil code is only a directive principle of State and is not enforceable. However, the distinction between Practice of essential or integral to a particular religion like Muslim Law is protected under article 25, a provision that seeks to preserve the freedom to practice and propagate any religion and these that go against to the concept of equality and dignity of which are Fundamental rights.

- Muslims in government: India has seen three Muslim Presidents and many Chief Minister of State Government.

Apart from this there are and have many Muslim Ministers, both at the Center and State level. Presidents like Zakir Hussain, Fakruddin Ali Ahmed, Dr. APJ Abdul Kalam. Vice President of India Mohammad Hamid Ansari former Minister Khurshid Ahmed and former Director (head) of the Indian Intelligence Bureau Syed Asif Ibrahim, Dr. Syed Qureshi served as Chief Election commission of India; Abid Husain, Ali Yaar Jung and Asif Ali Zafar Sultan Saifulla were cabinet Secretaries of the Government of India in 1993-94. Suleiman Hider was the former Secretary from 199-97. Influential Muslims personalities in India include Sheik Abdulla, son of Omar Abdulla former Chief Minister of Jammu and Kashmir, Mufti Muhammad? Sayeed, Sikandar Bakht, A.R. Antulay, C.H Mohammad Koya, Abdul GhaniKhan, Mukhtar Abbas Naqvi, Suleiman Khurshid, Saifuddin Soz, Ghulam Nabi Azad Syed Shaw Nawaz Husain and Asaduddin Owasi and amore among them.

- Indian Muslims and other minority communities have voting rights on par with Hindu majority.
- Film Industry Personalities include Dilip Kumar, Sharukh Khan, Salmann Khan, Amir Khan, Nasr Hussain, Irfan Khan, Salim Javed, Naushad, Mohammad Rafi, Talat Mahmoud, Madhubala, Nargis, Sham shad Begum, Roshan and many more among them.
- Hindu Film Personalities like Devanand, Raj Kapoor, B.R. chopra and Yash Chopra, N.C. Sippy and many number among they though they belong to Lahore Karachi which are now in Pakistan, they did not opt for partition.
- The irony is the Muslim are called as Vote Bank for the politicians who govern the India in general elections.
- To say in nutshell that the Muslim other minorities remained in India itself instead opting for partition, is Just because Indian Hindu respects and treat all humans as a man who have the soul of Hindus that is the humanity and humility. That is the Greatness of Generosity of India.

CHAPTER 13

THEN WHO, WE THE PEOPLE ARE

It has become a clear and naked truth that at the time Greek, Islamic and other European invasions India was the Earth's richest region for its wealth in precious and semi-precious stones, minarally, gold, silver; religiously Dharma and Non-violence and Tolerance and culturally in Arts and Fine Arts. Hindus at the time of invasions were unquestionably superior in more things than its neighboring countries like Chinese Persia, Sassanians, the Romans and the Byzantines of the immediate preceding centuries. They were the followers of Shiva and Vishnu on this sub-continent had created themselves a society more mentally evolved Joyous and prosperous too-than had been realized by Jews, Christians and Muslim Monotheists of the time. Medieval India until Islamic invasions which destroyed it was a history's most richly imaginative culture and one of the five most advanced civilizations of all times.

Look at the Hindu Art that Muslim fanatics severely damaged or destroyed. Ancient Hindu sculptures are still vigorous and sensual in the highest degree-more fascinating than human figurative art created anywhere else on the earth. But our sculptures rebuilt the same after the cooling down of the invasionary atrocities. No artist of any historical civilization has ever revealed the same genius as our ancient Hindustan's artists and artisans. Apart from Indias' intellectual and scientific achievement, the Indians as known to all nations for many centuries are the metal (essence) of wisdom,

the source of fairness and objectivity. They were the people of sublime pensiveness, Universal apologue… Indeed was snot a distinguished civilization as its achievements in Science, literature, Philosophy arts and architecture but also had distinguished itself for the invading Muslims in terms of its humanity, chivalry, tolerance and ethical surveillance.

We must not say that there were invasions and battles fought before and after the invasions. But it has its own code of conduct, method whereas the invasions of Muslims both lack method and ethical system. Though Hindu kings and prices of used to engage in wars, like in any major civilization of the time but such wars were relatively infrequent. Affirming his Muslim traveler Merchant Suleiman writes in his Sansilaut Towarikh (P.851) that 'the Indians used wars for conquest, but the occasions are rare.'

Indians used and still are observing high ethical conventions and behavior in times of both war and peace. Wars and battles were normally limited to martial class (Kshatriyas) of opposing parties, who used to clash mostly in open fields. They used to follow code of honor and *sacrificing* it for the sake of victory or material gain was *deemed a shame worse than death*. Muslim Historian Al-Idris wrote that Hindus never departed from justice. The religious teachers, priests, the commoners and civil servants and non-combatant particularly women, children and senior citizens were normally spared and saved and unmolested in wars. Religious symbols, establishments of religious monuments, temples churches, Mosques generally not attacked, pillaged and plundered war booty, a Major divinely sanctioned object of the Islamic holy war, was not a part of war and conquests in India. The women of the defeated side, were normally not captured or their chastity not violated.

The saying of Westerners that "Any thing is right both in love and war" is a meaningless and immoral hypothesis in the view of Indian Hindus. Everywhere there is a method even in madness also, it is just a Nature' Law and order. In short "In all her history of warfare, Hindu has few tales to tell of cities put to sword of the massacre of the non-combatants. Professor Arthur Basham (1986) stated that "To us most striking feature of the ancient civilization is its humanity and morality".

Hiuen Tsang, a seventh Century Buddhist pilgrim from China to Nalanda University recorded that the India, as country was little injured despite enough rivalries between the ruling princes of India" Another Chinese, Faxian a fourth century Pilgrim to India "marveled at the Peace and Prosperity and high culture of Indians. Having grown in the war-torn, Linda Johnson, says he was "deeply impressed by a land whose leaders were more concerned with promoting commerce and religion that with slaughter of substantial portion of the population. Another astonishing thing is the temperament that Hindu followed in terms the Historian Habibullah "was even though Muslims raided inhumanly Hindus treated Muslims with generosity and respect and allow them freedom, even to govern themselves." These ethical and tolerant Principles of Indias were tooted in its civilizational value system to treat humans whoever he may be, with humanity.

Even Asoka the exceptional personality for these moral and ethical standards adopted by Hindus, initially deviated from this code of ethics and tolerance in his ambition to become a great conqueror. However, finally he was left devastated by causalities that occurred in the conquest of a Kalinga, in which about 100,000 soldiers and commoners died. Subsequently he became a great humanist and used feel frightened by war, became a non-vegetarian, and vowed anti-war activist. He turned later non-violent and embraced Buddhism. He condoled himself for having committed a gross mistake against the Indian Dharma.

This transition is never seen in any of the Muslim and Europeans. Even they the Indian Hindus did pray their Lord for having allowed an opportunity to kill so many infidels as done by Babur Khilji and Gaznavides and Europeans like General Dyer.

The great Maratha King, who is noted for attacking Moghul Emperor Aurangzeb refrained from excessive bloodbath. When he attacked Surat, in 1634, its Moghul Governor Inayat Khan sent an envoy, to negotiate peace, in guise of which the envoy unsuccessfully fell upon Shivaji stood from the ground quickly and forbade massacre from the side Shivaji then approached that treacherous envoy and saluted a slap of courage to his back said "go tell to your King that Indian Kings never play a treachery. If you king want fight let him come face to face for combat and settle the war". That was a rare restraint showed by Indian Hindu Kings. This acts recalls us that Hindu is certainly belongs to the land of humanity, ethically behaved. Another example is that when Greek Warrior Alexander attacked the Porus the Indian counterpart of Sindh. Though Alexander was defeated, Porus blessed him to let off and "advised him to go back to his native place". He treated as equal to him though he is defeated in the battle. He treated him as guest and what all required to send him off to his native he arranged. This made Alexander to feel guilt and on account of this guilt he fell prey to depression and finally died on the way to his home.

Such is silent and salient command of the rare quality of Indian culture, philosophy and Religion irrespective of him being Indian or foreigner, enemy or friend. Indians are prepared to die for the same of preserving and protecting Dharma. This attitude made Idea made India reduced the population figure from 200 million to 170 million in 1500. Even then it never thought of taking revenge on the community that came and performed genocide of Indians for their selfish purpose and on account whose merciless act, the population got reduced.

Non-violence and tolerance are the major arsenals to combat with the enemy and he enemy out frustration and guilt of crime withdraw and leave the battlefield. Thus many of the foreign invaders were tired of the invasions posed a question –*what type of people you are*? You kill us without any sword or arrow? Besides this you show a smiling faces to meet the death penalty also and this became the cause of worry of suffering to the enemy psychologically? For this question Emperor to Commoner gave the reply with shortest sentence which speaks that "*We are Bharathia Hindus*". The more you cut the more we grow. The more you reject it the more we adapt it. *That is Hindu Dharma*.

CHAPTER 14

CONCLUSIVE REPORT ON THE ATROCITIES ARE STILL IN HEADWAY

The recent Report of 2016 Pathankot attack caused concern and I never expected that Pakistan will behave in such a in dignified way. It is like a back stabbing one's own mother. Let me narrate how inhuman the act of Pakistan who are supposed to extend their thanks for the gratitude the Hindu India has paid all the way.

The report made me to document few deteriorative suggestions to Government of India, the BJP Ruling Party so as to take the task of stern action and the report is that *"the 2016 Pathankot attack was a terrorist attack committed on 2nd January2016 by a heavily armed group which attacked the Pathankot Air command of the Indian Air Force. The gun battle and subsequent combing operation lasted about 17 hours on 2nd January, resulting in five attacks and three security personal dead. A further three soldiers died after being admitted in Hospital with injuries raising the death toll to six soldiers, On January 3rd fresh gunshots were heard and another Security Officer was gun downed by an IED explosion. The operation continued on 4th January and a fifth attack was confirmed killed. Not until a final terrorist was reported killed on 5th January was the anti-terrorist operation declared over though further searches continued for some time.*

Though the United Jihad council, a Kashmir based militant group claimed responsibility for the attack on 4th January, the attackers who were wearing Indian Army Fatigues were suspected to belong o Jaish-e-Muhammad an Militant group designated terrorist organization by India, the US,UK and UN.

The attack lead to the breakdown in India-Pakistan relations which remained largely unsolved as on June 2016. It is reports that the attack was an attempt to detail a fragile peace process meant to stabilize the deteriorated relations between and India and Pakistan. Pieces of evidence were found linking the attacks to Pakistan. Many of international countries including Afghanistan, US and UK condemned the attack. The President Barrack Obama strongly condemned the attack saluting the Indians who fought to prevent more loss of life. Tragedies like this also underscore why the US and India continue to be such close partners in fighting terrorism. He also described that ***"the Pathankot attack as another example of the inexcusable terrorism that India has endured too long"***

The big Terror attack in Pathankot threatens to derail a renewed Indian –Pakistan peace process. Already there had been successive attacks on 13 December 2001 on Parliament, New Delhi, causing the death of around 20 members including attackers, 2008 Mumbai attack referred to as 26/11 by terrorist's attack that took place in 2008 November when 10members of Lashkar-e- Toeba an Islamic organization based on Pakistan. They carried 12 coordinated shooting and bombing attack lasting four days in Mumbai which drew wide spread global condemnation on Wednesday 26 Nov 2008. Around 164 to 300 people died and wounded. Ajmal Kasab a young terrorist

caught by Indian police disclosed that the attack were the attackers were the member of Lashkar-e-Toeba and among others. Besides this already there had been successive attacks On Parliament on 13 December 2001, and daily attacks on Kashmir Border ever since 2017.

There are five reasons why India continue the process of talks announced after Bangkok and reaffirmed by the Prime Minister Narendra Modi in his meeting with Pakistan counter in Raiwind. Now the question arises as to why should we always have routine dialogue with Pakistan

Firstly, if there are no terror strikes emanating from Pakistan why would India need to talk to Pakistan anyway? India must confront Pakistan with an evidence of the use of its soil, perhaps even the support of its state institutions in terror attacks on India. It became a routine affair of dialogues, sitting on the table and ask them what about this? How can we normalize relations, when you do this? To call off talks would be walk away just when you need to confront, talk engage and seek answers.

Pakistan won't talk of terrorism until talks Kashmir and that is why we had a "composite dialogue "process whose name the Modi Government has changed to "Comprehensive dialogue". Since Kashmir has a line of control that is often a fire, and a source of Terrorist infiltration, India has a need to talk about Kashmir too.

Indian has no interest even in gaining Pakistan administered Jammu and Kashmir, although India talks about it when

Pakistan ratchet up its protestations an international border. It is Pakistan that has made training Indian administered Kashmir an article of faith. Pakistan's support to terrorism comes from the desire to Kashmir Valley, which it has not been able to gain military. Talking Kashmir and Terrorism, along with trade and Visas and everything else can bring Indian long term gains.

The **second step** must be we should be seen as that we want peace. We may never get to hear the details, but there has been much commentary in the press about the International pressure brought on India to talk to Pakistan. Washington and other world capitals want India to talk to Pakistan. Washington and other world capitals want India to talk to Pakistan because not talking often only escalates tensions, on the border and between the foreign offices in New Delhi and Islamabad. They fear this not only because it has serious implications for Washington's to contain Pakistan in Afghanistan, but also because both India and Pakistan are nuclear armed.

When India is not talking to Pakistan it comes across as the country that does not want to talk peace. Pakistan keeps saying it wants to talk to India without pre-conditions, India keeps saying what about terrorism and Pak say let us talk terrorism too. Instead of allowing itself to be seen as the one that does not want to sit down and talk to resolve issues, India should sit down and talk and let Pakistan be seen as the one that is up to terror strikes to derail talks. Talking to Pakistan is an opportunity to put the spot light as its India centric Terrorism infrastructure, not a way of forgetting terrorism.

Thirdly, we Indians lack military options. War is not an option for nuclear–armed neighbors but even short confrontation is out of question limited military action could easily escalate and even if it does not, what will it achieve if it does not, what will it achieve than making India look like aggressor? An air strike or two may not finish the terror infrastructure in Pakistan but will definitely create more anti-India Jihads. As Pakistan will continue to pretend it harbors no such elements, India has the capability to mount a "cold start" attack on Pakistan. It would be far easier to secure our border from terrorist infiltration instead. Indias lack military options and absence of sub-conventional warfare abilities mean that India has only one option left: diplomacy. Not talking is not diplomacy. Pakistan loses nothing by India not talking to it. It is only by talking and engaging that Indian can perhaps build some pressure on Pakistan. This is why "strategic restraint" has been key to India-Pakistan Policy.

Fourthly, one should "end the black mail" If terror strikes are aimed at halting India-Pakistan talks then why give the terrorists what they want? Why give into the black mail? The bully is why give into the black mail? They bully is emboldened every time you show him you were affected by the bullying. India appears stronger not weaker- if it continues to talk despite their bosses will know the trick is not working any more. By linking talks to incidents of terrorism India.

Fifthly and finally, working on Public opinion in both India and Pakistan. Now that hardline Prime Minister has been forced to talk to Pakistan and face the ignominy of terror strikes in response it is time to build broad political consensus that talking to Pakistan is in India's national self- interest and not same munificence towards Pakistan. Talks with Pakistan should be used as an opportunity by both sides to build public opinion for peace in both countries.

Doing so would be vial to isolating those who do not want normalization of relations such as terrorists and their supporters. Increased trade ties, for instance, can build a new constituency of peace backers with economic perception, once people see the other country as a living reality and not security monster of the news headlines. Similarly a long drawn out process of talks could be used to seek and shape Public opinion on out-of-the-box win-win solutions to issue such as Siachen and Kashmir.

When all the resources are exhausted, in my view, consult with both US and Russia and see that small war may be waged without using nuclear arms, and convert the Pakistan occupied Kashmir(POK) land into Indian land of Kashmir is back to

India. Peace, non-violence and tolerance the arsenals that were being practiced used Indian Hindu, need to be stripped off for the time being and see that the real armor that could sculpture the enemy into mendicant is the only method of last resort, as was done by former Prime Minister Indira Gandhi during 1971 by partitioning Pakistan into two halves with the concurrence of Super powers like UK, and US and Russia.

The appeasement of Pakistan should not be a policy option and India must employ verbal bellicosity and much flexing in its dealing with Pakistan when required. Failure to respond vigorously would surely encouraging more audacious adventurism by Pakistan. India should continue to engage Pakistan diplomatically monitoring careful the dynamics of the power equations between Army and civilian dispensation. The diplomacy must involve interaction with both the political and military leaders of the two countries.

It clearly stands out that India doesn't lack the ways and means to punish Pakistan either militarily or otherwise in case it continues to target India and create unrest and violence. Pakistan should know how we kindled on earlier occasions like Indira Gandhi who caused buttonhole of bifurcation of Pakistan in 1971. However, we Indians always stood for peaceful packages to avoid homicide of innocent civilians at both ends. Prudent demands that conventional military confrontation between two countries should never be allowed to escalate beyond a point and the use of nuclear weapons is not an option at all.

Some say in the way of peace method that there is need for India to develop a retaliation policies that should impose significant and escalating costs upon Pakistan diplomatically, politically and militarily without crossing critical threshold. India must also seek the intervention of the International community including US, UNO to compel Pakistan cease using terrorism as a state policy and military action by India which is instigated by the Pakistani adventurism must be supported by them. India must concentrate a strengthening its economy, military and homeland security and expedite police reforms, better intelligence coordination and hone capabilities to undertake covert operations behind enemy lines. India must also use all available regional leverages to influence the gouge behavior of Pakistan, having an adverbial effect on regional security. Concurrent efforts to improve economic and trade relations with Pakistan and regular cultural exchanges must be initiated to help build trust between the two nations. Both countries should initially harvest low hanging fruits like the Sir Creek disputes etc. enhance positively before resolving the more sensitive issues. India must also continue to reiterate its claim on POK (Pakistan occupied Kashmir) and remind the international community at every available opportunity that POK is a legitimate part of the Indian Union that is under the illegal occupation of the Pakistan. The blatant violence of human rights deliberately keeping the region in a state of abject poverty illiteracy and backwardness needs to find mention in all international fora by India.

However, the issue of confrontation with Pakistan is going to maturate year after year and on account of which our Jawan's and innocent public are being laid down to death or impaired for the no reason to attribute. This type of reaction from Indian peace lovers would indemnify to the large scale supporters of Pakistan. Whenever the Hocky or Cricket is played between India and Pakistan, a high-tension Tsunami wave blows in both the Muslims of Indian and Pakistan. There is a saying that "If Pakistan sneezes the virus is felt in Indian Muslims". This projects the doubt that are Indian Muslim brothers are really Indian or Pakistani" Such is the trend prevailed among the Indian Muslims ever since the partition supervened. I being a Muslim whenever I comment on such occasions with fellow Muslims of India the immediate rebuff will be "Why are you negating the Pakistan? Are you not Muslim? If you are a Muslim you should extend your support to Muslim brothers wherever they live. All Muslims should hate and smite Idolaters. It is the duty of Muslims to hate Kafirs". They argue that "You are in support of idolaters who are Kafirs then you are a mujahidin who would be the first man to be killed or out casted as ordered by our Prophet Muhammad". This ideology need to amputate off. Even in Mosques while praying and praising the God the Imam make a plea to **whack non-believers from the globe.** This is the internal problem we are facing. Our Indian Muslims are our enemies first and hence they need to be repatriated back to Pakistan as a residual refugees.

Mahatma Gandhi has once referred that Muslims are bullies and Hindus are cowardice. As a matter fact he himself fought for Independence through non-violence which is the standing example for cowardice. Gandhi himself supported Chandrasekhar Azad who was prepared to fight Independence movement through valor and courage, for which Gandhi himself fail to accept and did not cooperate the violent methods adopted Mr. Azad. Then Gandhi himself guilty of cowardice act rather strong leader. Perhaps Gandhi might have thought that the getting of Independence movement through non-violence may fail its agenda and the credit of obtaining Freedom through non-violent process may be lost and getting freedom through violence and aggressive process will be granted by British India. It so because that the British have tiered themselves for having lost much of their exchequer in the Second World War they are about to grant the independence at any cost and at any moment. And this Gandhi wanted to encash and assigned the credit of Independence through Ahimsa process and get credit for himself. He never wanted to see others get and gain the independence through non-violent process and his name would be written in golden letters in the History of India. That was the reason he failed to get Nobel laureate. That is why he spoken on some occasion that Muslims are bullies and Hindus are cowardice. In above section of this treatise you would have come across the mention of invasions of Muslims since 1400 years. Very few Shivaji's and Maharana Pratap's who played pivotal role in counter attacking the bloody invasions and which were fought through valor and courage.

Gandhi may be right in saying that Hindus are cowards. There has been in the past 1400 years since the first invasion started, very few Shivaji's and Maha Rana Pratap's to fight the bloody role of Moghuls or hardly Rani Jhansi's fight to stand against humiliating colonial yoke of British. If a nations souls measured by the courage of its children, then India is definitely doomed without the Sikhs whose bravery is unparalleled, in the more recent history of India, Hindus would have even lost addition land to the Muslims invaders and there would have been infinitely more massacred of Hindus by Muslims during the first weeks of Partition. Are the Hindus more courageous when they have an independent India now? Not at all. Because of Nehru's absurd and naïve "Hindi –China Bhai-Bhai policy, the Indian army was shamefully routed in 1962 by the Chinese, a humiliation which rankles even today. Beijing is still able to hoodwink Indian politicians by pretending it has good intentions, while quietly keeping on giving nuclear know-how to Pakistan as well as the Missiles to carry their atomic tests where as to Indian cities arm separatists group in North East and continuing to claim Arunachal Pradesh or Sikkim.

Today we see that Indian politicians, instead of standing up to Islamic militancy and Chinese bully, prefer to look the other way and speak of "Hindu Terrorism", an absurdity if there is one. Hindus are hounded , humiliated, routed be it in Pakistan and Bangladesh, where Muslims indulge in programs against a Hindus every time they want vent their hunger against India (as pointed out by Tasleem Nasreen's book Lajja). In Kashmir the land of Yogis, where Hindu Sadhus and sages have meditated for 5000 years. Hindu have been chased out of their ancestral home by death, terror and intimidation. There were 25 % of Hindus the beginning of the century in the Kashmir Valley… and hardly handful to day. And look how the U.S is treating India, refusing to Handover Headly responsible for the planning of the horrible Mumbai attacks and continuing to prop-up Pakistan, knowing very well when American troops will leave Afghanistan, Islamabad will make sure that a friendly Taliban regime is reinstated with dire consequences for India's security.

There is no point in playing against Pakistan as long as Islamabad is sending militants to kill and maim into territory. Yet Hindus continue to think that in the name of sportsmanship or democracy. It is right thing to do. We keep hearing about Hindu terrorism. But since fourteen centuries, Muslims have always struck first against Hindus. And those who live in Indian cities which have important Muslim minorities, will tell you that every time there are Hindu Muslims, if the Muslims who start them either by attacking the Police or by provoking the Hindus.

The truth is one there is one standard in India: one for the Hindus and one for Muslims. Did the "Fanatic" Hindus who brought down Ayodhya (and brought shame on to secular India, according to the Indian media) kill or even injure anyone in the process? No but Muslims do not have such qualms. When Gandhi said they were bullies, he was being very nice or very polite. For forget about the millions of Hidus killed the ten century of Muslims invasions probably the worst holocaust in the World's History; forget about the hundreds thousands of Hindu temples razed to the ground, whose distruction what ever our secular Hindus of today say –was carefuylly recorded by the Muslims themselves, because they were proud of it or proud of such individuals like Aurangazeb whose goal was to eraze Kafirs from the facet of the Earth. Forget about the millions Hindus forcebly converted into Islam and who sadly are rallying now under banner, a language or scripture which have nothing to do with their own ethos and culture. Yesterday and also today, when the Muslim world feels it has been slighted, in even small measures by Hindus these infidels who sumitted meeky to Muslimrule for tencenturies, it retaliates a hundred fold-this is the only way one intimidates cowards. Ayodhya, Pakistan, Saudi Arabia (at least in Passive by giving shelter for a while to Tiger Memon) while they help Indian Muslims planted bombs in the heart of Bombay and killed a thousand innocent human beings most of them are once more Hindus.

This is no to say that Muslims are fanatic on the contrary, many of India's Muslims are extremely gentle and their sense of hospitality unsurpassed. The same thing cane said about Pakistan: Pakistan Politicians for instances are made more accessible than India. Pakistan has its own identity, which cannot be wished away. No the problem is not within Muslims whether they are Indians or Pakistanis, the problem is with Islam which teaches Indian Muslims from an age to look beyond their national identity to a country the Mecca in Saudi Arabia-which is not their country, to read a scripture which is not written in their own language to espouse a way of thinking, which is inimical to their own roots and indigenous culture. Indian Muslims have to think of themselves first as an Indian and secondly only as Muslims. Muslims soldiers fighting against Pakistan in Kargil, have shown the way.

Yes. Culture of Hindus, the way they respected each other's vision, the way they admitted theories the way they lived always led them to peace. Hindu never accept the brutality of killing someone because of his different ideology, culture and the way of living Hindu who fought for their rights meant no harm to the culture of the lives of the people. Hindu kings who fought with each other never agreed to harm the people and their culture they used to perform. Their women were not raped, their men not slaughter their children were not abducted as sex slaves. But after Islamic invasion, brutality took place as a major agenda all over the lands of Hindus on the name of Allah and Religion.

When Muhammad bin Qasim invaded India a new way of living introduced according to Islam. But Hindus were strong and they did not easily agree to follow other religion than them. When Islam rulers started to force the conversion, Hindu raised how the brutality started against as "Religious war". It is not fact that Hindu's were not fools to understand the "the new way" of living, it is just ideology and religion beliefs they had been from thousands of years after the birth of other religious beliefs.

Hindus believed in discussion of theological topics and they never intended to kill any one for difference of opinions. Hindu never imposed their ideologies on others. But, when invaders ascended the throne they invaded circumstances of Hindu religious beliefs too. A series of attack from outlanders of brutality and the patience of Hindu emperor inculcated the wrong assumption that Hindus is coward. Does they change their beliefs? Does they sit at home as coward?

And the answer is No.

Till this day, those brutality, ideology of true faith *"ideology to kill"* people on the name of Religion is going on. And in Islam, it preaches that "Those who do not believe in Islam and its revelation shall be inherited to hell

Hindus believed in their ideology that preaches of *Vasudaiva Kutumbam*—the world is one family where it reaches Humanity. *Athithi Devobhava* –the guest is equivalent to God" which preaches the culture. From thousands years, the land of Hindu been preaching the lessons of non-violence, to entire world. It is not the sign of cowardice of Hindu who blindly accept, but to the certain tolerance of Hindu blood. After all there hundreds of invasions, terrorist attacks conversions and those betrayals survived. After all these brutalities on Hindu people, Hindu still survived. Do you call it a "Cowardice"?

Amaranth at Baatengo, Ananthnag District on the basis of same ideology "Religious War Fare". Seven of them died and eighteen severely wounded. Claimed that it is a retaliation of Terrorists with the reason of three LTE men's arrest

One would be tempted to say that stop being cowards remember that a nations requires Kshatriyas warriors, to defend knowledge to protect one's own women and children to guard one's borders from the enemy. And do Indians need a Narender Mode to remind them of that simple truth?

Those who are still campaigning on the name of 'Religious warfare" should remember one fact that to the certain extent,

Hindu follow the first verse "***Ahimsa Paramo Dharma***" (Non-violence is the greatest duty of a Hindu) but series of attacks questions their ego they will follow the next that preaches "***Dharma Himsa thathiwacha***"(It is duty of a Hihdu counter the violence by violence in defense of one's self.)

Hindus believed in Ancient preaches that say non-violence is ultimate Dharma (duty), so too is violence in service of dharma' as Arjuna in Mahabharata was advised by Lord Krishna.

They always ***supportive*** of whatever small action Pakistan/ Muslim does. Even it is a matter of anti-India no matter and they feel happier for abusing Indian Hindu. The time is mellowed to spare these people to deport to their neighbor friends that is Pakistan or else a day will come that We Hindu Indians have to get extricated and our name plate of India on the map of ***Hindustan*** would be replaced as ***Muslimistan*** in retribution of time. Then we can say that: ***WE the Hindu Indian people can retaliate any combat that come across*** as Porus did with Alexander and Shivaji with Aurangzeb and Azaad and Gandhi with British in the past History. We can create new History too as our youth have become the cognizant of the augmentation of the damages fabricated by the foreign invaders including monotheistic communities. This would be last triumph card that needs to be thrown against Pakistan and settle the issue finally.

That is the reply for the question that "who are, we the people"?

REFERENCES

1	Boston A.G	-The Legacy of Jihad "Islamic holy and the fate of the Non-Muslims Prometheus Book New York 2005
2	Khan M.A	Islamic Jihad: A legacy forced conversion imperialism and slavery-Universe Bloomington In 2009
3.	Lal. K.S.	Muslim Invade India P.433, 453 - Boston
4.	Lal. K.S.	The Origin of Muslim slave system Page 529-534
5.	Lal. K.S.	Enslavement of Hindus by Arab and Turkish invasions P. 549-554.
6.	Lal. K.S.	Jihad under Turks and Jihad under Moghuls
7.	Ahmed bin Naquin	Reliance Traveler: A classic Manual of Manual sacred Law. In Arabic with facing English Text translated by Nuh Hamim, Al Misri
8.	Sookh Dev. P	Global Jihad. The Future in the face of Islam-Isaac Publishing 2007
9	Mariam Kohen-David Littman	Ye or Bat-Islam "Dhimmitude-Where civilization collide"-Fair Leigh Dickinson University Press 2002 Reprinted 2005
10	Stephen Knap	The Real History of India-Its Heroes and Invaders
11	Francois Gautier	Arise Again O India-2005
12	John Briggs	Ferhista Mohammad Khasim-Hindu Shah translation 1825-1981 Tariq –E-Ferhista
13	Miller Sam	A third Intermission of –A strange kind of Paradise-India Through Foreign Eye-2014-Random House P.80
14	L.K. Saran	1999-Theory and Practice of State in India Research Publication-p.89
15	Digby Simon	Bulletin of the School and African Studies-University of London Vol. 38 P.no.1-1975.
16	Andre Wink	Al-Hind the making of the Indo-Islamic world –Early Medieval India and the Expansion of Islam-7th and 11th centuries Brill P.161 (2002)

17	Elst Koenaraad	The Ayodhya Debate in Gilbert Pellet-India Epic Values-Ramayana and its Impact-1991-Peters Publisher p.33
18	The New Indian Express	Goa Inquisition -Most merciless and cruel 2016-5-17
19	Rao R.P	Portuguese Rule In Goa-Asia Publishing House 1963
20	Alan Machado Prabhu	Saraswathis' Children
21	Wikipedia	History and Timeline of Independence
22	Yasmin Khan	The Great Partition: Making of India and Pakistan University press: 2007
23	Pak Times	Two Nation Theory –Achieved from original 11th November 2007
24	Jain.J. Chandra	Gandhi-A Forgotten Mahatma—Mittal publication-p.38-1987
25	Springer	-Population Re-distribution and Development in South Asia-Science & Business-March 2012
26	Peter Garter	The Making of Modern Refugee –Oxford University Press-pp149
27	Sohail Riaz	Hindus Feel The Heat in Pakistan-March 2007-Retrived in 2011
28	New York Times	Pakistani Attack 30 Hindu Temples –1991 December
29	Abbas Zafar	Journalists find Baluchistan War Zone
30	Sahautara Naeem	Hindus Pakistan being Denied access to Temples-Excess Tribune-New York
31	Nayyar.A & Salim. A	The Subtle Subversion –A Report on Curricula and Text Books In Pakistan
32	Arivndan Banerjee	"Noor's Cure"-A contrast views-2003- Rediff: India and Abroad 2010
33	Sharma Arvind	Classical Hindu Thought-New Delhi Oxford University press-2000
34	Mittal Sushil and Thorsby	Gene (2004) the A Hindu World New Work Routledge Press
35	Source of Images	Indian Partition-and-Annexation Hyderabad-Wikipedia

About The Author

I am a simple man, retired as Office in the Office of the Accountant General Hyderabad, I did my Ph.D. and L.L.B after retirement at the age of 70. I do not believe Creation was caused by any God or super Spirit since no animal including Human being do have a spirit called "Soul" It is the activity of our Brain that every animal including humans possessed. That is the thing that Humans "Social Animal" or "Intelligent Animal" I believe the theory of Evolution of Natural selection which was first formulated by Charles Darwin in his Book" *On the Origin of Species* in 1859, and is the process by which organs change overtime and as a result of change inheritable Physical or behavioral traits takes shape. I also believe that there is no necessity of any God to take up the creation and thereby expect Man and woman for prostrating him for life time. If any god who have a desire to submit and give Credit to him is a whisper and that is none other a humanly emotion, is not a God but **human itself**. And this connotes that the Religion and God are the creations human for tackling his fear and ambition.